Praise f

Kind, But Kind of Weird

Kind, But Kind of Weird is a fabulous collection of stories, combining quirky humor with a curiosity toward the world around us. These short narratives take you on a journey leaving you both giggling and pondering the meaning of life. And it'll make you more observant the next time you go out—if only to see what kind of strange experiences you come across.

—Carrie Bohlig
Author of *So You Want to Start a Side Hustle*,
Owner of Tandem Consulting, Founder of Tandem Giving

Kind, But Kind of Weird is a perfect accessory for a hammock and a well-mixed gin & tonic. Held brings his variety of relatable characters to everyday experiences, but makes them exponentially more entertaining than would be experienced in the moment. Highly entertaining, short, thoughtful, and often hilarious stories that will keep you turning pages until you finish your cocktail . . . or two.

—Sarah Elkins
Author of *Your Stories Don't Define You,
How You Tell Them Will*

The author delivers a masterclass in the art of short storytelling, with this insightful and thoroughly satisfying study of the human condition, in all its whimsical and poignant glory.

—Craig Leener
Author of *The Zeke Archer Basketball Trilogy*

A wittily insightful collection of stories that charms on the surface, with Joey's creative hand and a heaping spoonful of clever wordplay, yet on a deeper level are an often-poignant commentary on the human condition. Don't be surprised if you find yourself reflected in these stories, either with a smile or a forkful of humble pie. An at once fun and thoughtful perspective on everyday situations and life's quirky conundrums.

—Stacey Aaronson
Writer, editor, and founder of
The Book Doctor Is In

These short stories are a culmination of Joey's innate curiosity and positive perspective on life. The worlds and characters that Joey has dreamed up are delicious to the senses, and I dream to see one of these short stories on the big screen!

—Annette Silva
Television Producer

Delightful, engaging, and human from beginning to end. A strong exploration of the various relationships we encounter throughout our lives, with each main character unique, but always a little familiar. You never know who you're going to meet next!

—Tayler Gill
Remote Work and Traveling Coach,
Founder of Traveling Tayler

When they say a book can paint a picture in your head, they were totally talking about *Kind, But Kind of Weird*. Page by page, I caught Joey's words painting an all too relatable picture. From creatures to human characters, I found myself loving the character development in such short pages.

—Claire Saldaña
Commercial & Personal Stylist

Joey is—just like this book—kind, but kind of weird. He's also a brilliantly funny, awesome person, and given that I generally dislike 99% of people, that's saying something. Do yourself a favor: Buy this book and get comfy, because this is a collection you'll want to read in one sitting. (And then over and over again.)

—Traci Koller Mazurek
Founder, Delancey Collective

This delightful series of unique stories provides perfectly sized mental vacations for those short on attention span and in need of a break from the backlit social media scandals of the day. Joey takes seemingly uncommon situations and infuses them with familiar exchanges and emotions as you travel through the curiously concocted tales.

—S. Kolaczkowski
Miss Coach K

I've known Joey since college and that same student who was witty, creative, passionate, and drop-dead funny definitely shines through this book. I'm so glad that his storytelling is no longer unique to me, but now available to the world. The reader will certainly get a kick out of this book, with short stories to pass on to their grandchildren.

—Sean
Twitch Streamer, seanyboy05

Kind, But
Kind of Weird

Kind, But Kind of Weird

Short Stories on Life's Relationships

JOEY HELD

Cover design by Tabitha Lahr
Interior text design by Backstory Design

PB ISBN: 978-0-578-30242-3
Also available as an eBook.

10 9 8 7 6 5 4 3 2 1

To Mom, Dad, Elizabeth, Haleigh, Franxie, and Merlin.

Also, the haters.

Contents

Kind, But
Kind of Weird

Withering on Withersby Road

"NO, IT'S NOT SAYING TAKE A LEFT. IT MEANS *BEAR* LEFT," MEGAN said. "You know, like on that diagonal street there."

"That can't be it. That's still basically straight," I said.

"Look, if you had charged your stupid phone, we wouldn't be in this mess," Megan said. "You know this GPS is a piece of junk."

"And if *you* had a phone made in this century, you'd have GPS on your phone," I shouted. "Instead, we're stuck with this stand-alone thing my parents got me as my main Christmas gift the year I got my license. Sorry."

As usual, we were late. This time it was my fault. I'd been trying to find the perfect pocket square to impress my friend Brandon's dad. Brandon was the one getting married, and his father was a designer of pristine ties, pocket squares, kerchiefs, and other fashion accessories. Mr. Tallman was a good guy to know for a freelance writer hoping to break into the fashion industry.

Problem was, I only owned two pocket squares: a checkered blue and silver one and a striped blue and silver one. I've never been strong at making quick decisions, especially when they carried a lot of weight. Picking between the two pocket squares was an agonizing choice, and it ended up being one of the main reasons we were now running late to this wedding.

The other reason was that the directions were absolutely awful. We plugged in the address on my antiquated GPS, and after about eight minutes of locating the satellite signal, it had finally found the location, but was not making it easy on us.

"Wait, was that Witherly Road back there?" I asked, my eyes scanning the rearview mirror. I was hoping to read the street sign we had just passed, but I couldn't make it out.

"I'm sorry, what did you say?" Megan asked. "I'm trying to jump ahead in these directions. We take a left on Witherly, and then it's straight for half a mile, then a quick right through the forest preserve, a U-turn at the eleventh tree, a right on Morgansview Drive, go through seven traffic circles, and finally the church will be on our left. Have we passed Witherly Road yet?"

"That's what I just asked!" I yelled. I made a U-turn without looking at oncoming traffic at all. The blaring horn of an eighteen-wheeler let me know that behavior was not acceptable. I gave a little wave and hoped he forgave me.

We drove back through the light we had passed a few minutes earlier. After a more careful U-turn, this time making sure traffic had dissipated, we headed back south toward Witherly Road. Or rather, to Withersby Road, which is what this street sign said. We pulled up to the intersection at a red light.

"Do you think this is it?" I said. "Is it just a typo?"

"I don't know," Megan said. "I can't see Withersby on the map. Maybe it's the same thing?"

"What do you think we should do, then?"

"I don't know!" Megan said. "I've never been to this part of town before."

"Me neither," I said. "Let's just keep going. I'm sure there's a Witherly somewhere down the road. What does the GPS say, anyway?"

"It says, 'Satellite Error' and currently has our car in the middle of the Pacific Ocean."

"That's very helpful," I said. "Can you at least move around and see the map? Maybe we can manually do it."

Megan pushed a button, and the GPS began screaming in Spanish at us.

"Make it stop!" I yelled. "It's so loud!"

Frantically, Megan pressed the screen, trying to get back into English mode, if nothing else. She held down the power button and even tried to unplug the GPS entirely. But the directions were still being blasted into our eardrums at maximum volume, and worse, in a language neither of us understood.

"Do something, Megan!" I said. "I cannot drive like this!"

With an exasperated scream, Megan rolled down the window and tossed the GPS into the street. A trio of cars drove over it, and none of them stopped to see what they had just destroyed. Maybe they were all going to the same wedding, too.

I gave Megan a sideways glance. "What?" she said. "It's not bothering you anymore, is it?"

"Good point," I said. "But now we have no idea where Witherly is. Can you take out the physical map from the glove compartment?"

"Sure, but I haven't read a map in . . . uh, maybe ever," she said, unfolding the paper in front of her no fewer than nine times.

"That's still more recently than the last time I read one," I said. "I know we're kind of near the lake. That's about it."

"You're aware the lake is huge, right?" she shot back. "That's not helpful at all."

"Look, I don't want to argue," I said. "Just see if you can figure out where we are. The ceremony starts in ten minutes."

"You don't need to yell at me," she said. "I'm looking for this stupid Withersby, and it doesn't help that we keep driving, so I don't know where we are now anyway."

She made a valid argument. I pulled into a gas station on the side of the road. "You know what?" I said. "Why don't I ask the gas station attendant in here? He'll probably know where we need to go."

"Good idea," Megan said. "I could use a little breathing room, anyway."

That seemed like an unnecessary dig, but I was in too much of a hurry to counter it. Inside the convenience store, the attendant was helping a woman who was buying an uncomfortable number of salted snacks. Peanuts, chips, pretzels, sour gummy worms—the whole works. I was impressed she could even carry everything out of the place.

I headed to the soft drink machine at the back of the store. To increase my chances of the attendant being friendly, I decided I'd buy a drink. If nothing else, it would thank him for his troubles.

The entire place seemed to be coated with a thin film of grime. I ran my hand over a shelf; when I pulled it away, my fingertips were stained black. Luckily, there was a beat-up paper towel roll by the drink machine. I yanked a piece off to wipe my hands. Whatever that black substance was tarred up the paper towel. Somehow, even though my fingers were now clean, my hand still felt sticky.

I picked up the smallest cup, which was sixty-four ounces. I figured that must be a mistake but nope. Oh, well. Possibly contracting diabetes after drinking a bucket of soda this store labeled "small" was the least of my worries. I filled the cup up with something called "Mango Tango," a drink I had never heard of. It was an unusual burnt orange color. I'm not particularly a fan of mango, but the little logo had a mango slow dancing with a banana. That was enticing enough to try it.

"Hello, sir!" I said with way too much enthusiasm as I stepped up to the counter. "We're on our way to a wedding, and we're unfortunately a bit lost. Maybe you could help?"

"I was wondering what you was doing all buttoned up like that," he said. When he spoke, only a small corner of his mouth moved. The rest stayed locked airtight. "Makes a lotta sense now. What can I do you for?"

"We're looking for Witherly Street," I said. "We passed a Withersby earlier, but that's not the same thing, is it?"

"Aw, yeah, Witherly," he said, rubbing his chin as he thought. "That doggone street is gonna be the death of this town, I tell you something. Here's the thing: Witherly don't exist no more. It got renamed a few years back. The dumb old technology ain't caught up yet."

"That would explain it!" I said. "What's the new name of the street?"

"New name is Witherly," he said.

"I'm sorry, that . . . that sounds like the street you said was renamed? What's the new name?"

"Just told you it," he said. "You hard of hearing out there?"

"No, sir, it simply seems like you said 'Witherly' again, so I wanted to make sure I had the name right." My hand was starting to shake from the weight of the Mango Tango. I'm not sure why I hadn't put it down, but it was too late now.

"Naw, you dingus. I said 'With-AR-lee.' With an 'a.' Keep going a couple blocks east, then it'll be there, with a statue of a sea turtle on your left. You can't miss it."

"Oh, that sounds wonderful," I said, pulling two dollar bills out of my pocket. "Keep the change!"

I headed to the door when I heard him clear his throat. "Now where in tarnation you think you're going, partner?"

I tilted my head toward him, confused. "What do you mean?"

"You're still fitty-nine cents short. You got a small, which is two dollars and fitty-nine cents. Don't make me get angry and have to shake you down, now."

"Oh, I didn't realize! I'm sorry, my mistake," I said. I tried to fish out sixty cents from the zippered compartment of my wallet, but after a few minutes I realized I only had two dimes in there. "Actually, can I put it on my card?"

"Five dollar minimum for credit," he said, pointing to a dusty sign on the wall. The writing looked like it had been done by a six-year-old. I looked at the man's curled, gnarly hands and realized he may have been the sign's calligrapher.

"Hmm, okay," I said. I hated the idea of getting something else, but with mere minutes until the wedding, there was no time to be cheap. "How about a pack of gum here?"

"One more dollar," he said.

"Okay, and . . . a copy of *Snagg'd*." *Snagg'd* was a magazine I had heard my friend Micah talking about. It featured these cool pictures of animals and humans snagging things. In any given issue, you could see a bird plucking a fish out of the sea, a baseball outfielder robbing a batter of a home run, or a bear reaching its paw into a cookie jar. Micah subscribed to the magazine and loved it, so I figured checking out an issue wouldn't hurt. Besides, I'd have something to page through if the wedding reception was really boring.

The attendant looked surprised that the store even carried such a magazine but brought it over for me. "All right then, your total is seventeen dollars and eighty-one cents." I guess I had slightly underestimated how much a magazine would cost. I handed my card to the attendant, who rang it up and told me good luck.

I got back into the car. Megan was glaring at me. "What could have possibly taken you so long?" she said. "I thought you were only going in there for directions."

"Oh, you know how it is," I said. "You go in thinking you're just going to ask for directions, and before you know it—"

"You have a copy of *Snagg'd?*" Megan said. "What even is this magazine?"

"It's Micah's favorite!" I said. "He subscribes to it."

"Isn't that a surprise?" Megan said, rolling her eyes. She wasn't a big fan of Micah, mostly because one time during a potluck dinner he spilled an entire green bean casserole on her. Though in his defense, that could have been anyone slipping on a wet floor. He simply happened to be the one to walk right over the most slippery part. "Did you find out where the street is?"

"Yeah, it got renamed, apparently," I said. "But it's still basically the same thing . . . I'll explain later. Just keep your eyes open for a sea turtle." Megan looked at me like I was growing a horn out of my forehead. I touched a hand up there, just in case. Nothing yet.

A few blocks later, we saw what appeared to be the sea turtle statue we had been looking for. It was tiny, maybe only a foot and a half tall, and we certainly would have missed it if there hadn't been a long line at the traffic light. That gave us enough time to scan our surroundings. It must have been my eyes playing tricks on me, but I thought I saw the sea turtle statue flap its legs, almost as if it were guiding us to Witharly.

I took a left and sped down the street. A church appeared on the right, so I turned into the parking lot and grabbed the first spot I saw. "Let's go!" I yelled to Megan, who was still gathering her purse. "We're already late!"

We ran up to the glass doors and could hear the organ playing inside. I held the door for Megan. "Come on, grab any seat," I said. The rear rows were taken, probably by people who were hoping to make an early exit. We slunk into a pew three rows from the back, next to a middle-aged couple.

"Do you see any of our friends?" Megan asked. "Honestly, I don't even recognize a single person here."

"They're probably all at the front," I whispered back. "You know how they like to have a good view. We'll catch up with them after the ceremony."

The organ music continued, and everyone rose to their feet. As we turned to face the beautiful bride, Megan elbowed me in the ribs. "That's not Amanda," she whispered to me. "I've never seen that girl before in my life."

"Are you sure?" I said. "We don't know her very well."

"*You* might not, but I've spoken with her every time we go out with her and Brandon," Megan said. "She's really a nice woman. Try talking to her sometime."

"Hmm, maybe it's new makeup or something," I said, scratching my head. "It's gotta be her."

"I'm telling you, it's not," Megan said. "Don't you ever listen?"

The woman in front of us turned around, an annoyed look on her face. I didn't recognize her either.

Amanda had already passed by, so we turned our attention to the altar. That's when I first noticed the groom. It wasn't Brandon. It wasn't even close. This guy was probably a good foot shorter than Brandon. And his hair was blond, not brown. And he had a beard.

I leaned over to Megan. "I think you're right," I said. "That's not Amanda. And she's certainly not about to marry Brandon. I'm beginning to believe we're at the wrong wedding."

"Duh," Megan said. "I figured that out already. But what do we do? We can't leave, can we?"

"That does seem like a rude move," I said. "Maybe we can duck out really quick when everyone turns back around to the front? There are only a few rows behind us—they probably wouldn't mind."

Just as I said that, another couple and their three children sat down next to us, effectively blocking our exit path. One of the kids immediately started punching my leg.

"Oh, don't mind little Caleb," the little monster's mother said.

"He's going through one of those phases where he thinks everything is punchable."

I gave my best fake smile and turned back to Megan. "There goes that idea. Maybe we just stay here, and we'll catch up with everyone at the reception?"

"Okay," Megan said. "She does have a beautiful dress. I'm sure the ceremony will be lovely."

She was right. It was a terrific ceremony. The bride and groom, who we discovered were named Whitney and Zack, both seemed like cool people with a genuine love for each other. Megan dabbed at her eyes with my pocket square, and for a moment I forgot all about the reason I had that pocket square in the first place.

After the ceremony, we moved down the receiving line. Megan sped through, briefly shaking everyone's hand. I was a little bit slower, not wanting to seem rude. Whitney's dad gave me a big hug, and Zack's mom clutched at my hands like they held treasure. "You're such a good friend, coming all the way out here to support the happy couple," she said, beaming at me. Did she somehow know what we had gone through? "So special seeing such a loving community celebrating with us."

I continued down the line, shaking hands and smiling at everyone I encountered. Most of them expressed a look of unfamiliarity toward me. At the end of the line, Zack and Whitney turned toward me. They shared a confused glance.

"I'm sorry, but who are you?" Zack asked.

"Me?" I asked, looking around. "I'm a good friend of Brandon's."

"Who's Brandon?" Whitney asked.

"The groom in the wedding we're supposed to be at. Do you know if there's another church around here?"

Megan grabbed me by the shoulders and dragged me out of the church. It was like getting the hook at the Apollo.

"Hey, I've got Micah on the phone," Megan said. "He was the only one who picked up."

She nodded as she listened to the voice on the other end, occasionally peppering the conversation with an "uh huh" or "okay." As the call went on, her face gradually became more contorted as she scrunched up her nose and furrowed her brow. After a couple of minutes, she thanked Micah and hung up.

"What did he say?" I asked.

"Turns out we were supposed to turn at Withersby Road," Megan said. "The correct church is like a minute away from that intersection."

"Huh, maybe we should have done a practice run yesterday," I said. "Do you remember how to get back to that intersection?"

Sheriff Shrimp

AT THE BOTTOM OF SCAMPI BAY LIVED A SMALL POPULATION OF aquatic creatures. They had developed a nice little town, full of things you'd find in any neighborhood. Lenny the Lobster had opened up a pool hall, which, as far as he knew, was the first of its kind in the deep sea. He served tasty cocktails, like Seaweed Sunrises and Bubble Teas. Not only could patrons come in and play pool, they could also go swimming in the outdoor area.

Then, of course, there was Gabbie's Groceries. Gabbie was a lantern fish who had set up shop a few years earlier. Guests could always spot her at the entrance, greeting customers who came in and making sure they had no trouble finding anything. Gabbie was rarely out of stock of any supplies. Oddly enough, though, her sign, which was illuminated every minute of the day, almost always had at least one letter burnt out.

While the residents went about their routines, Sheriff Shrimp oversaw the entire town. Each morning he'd wake up, put on his brown boots, slip his sheriff's jacket on, adjust the badge so it had the slightest tilt of authority, and put on his hat. Sheriff Shrimp wasn't a very large creature, but he walked with a sense of purpose. The other townscreatures respected him for that. In fact, since he became sheriff, murder via digestion had decreased by nearly forty percent.

Sheriff Shrimp liked to go from home to home and pay visits to the townscreatures. He wanted everyone to be able to put a face to the sheriff. The previous head of the town had been an octopus, who would often blend into his surroundings, waiting until someone was doing something illegal before revealing himself and capturing the poor unsuspecting criminal. This practice led to a real sense of unease in Scampi Bay, so Sheriff Shrimp set out to do the opposite of that. His aim was to get to know every single creature in town, and he was coming pretty darn close to doing so.

He just had one final row of homes to visit. It was a quartet of abodes composed of rocks aligned in geothermal crevices that sat along a small ledge in a corner of the bay. Sheriff Shrimp set off on the strenuous swim he had in front of him.

An hour later, he arrived at the first home, which was inhabited by a mama and papa plankton and a small baby girl plankton. The whole family was milling about in the yard, swimming back and forth in frenetic fashion.

"Good afternoon!" Sheriff Shrimp bellowed across the water. For such a small creature, he sure did have a deep voice.

"Hello, Sheriff!" the mama plankton squeaked back. "It's lovely to see you up here. So good that you get out and meet all the townscreatures."

"Just doing my job, ma'am," Sheriff Shrimp said, reaching up and tipping his hat ever so slightly. "How's your day been treating you?"

"Oh, it's just lovely!" the mama plankton squeaked. "We're about to head out to the farmer's market in the town square. Little Planchette is so excited."

Sheriff Shrimp looked at the baby plankton, who was skipping around the adults, singing "la la la" at the top of her little baby lungs. Sheriff Shrimp crouched down next to her. "Ready for your first trip to the market?" he asked.

"Oh yes, sir!" the little baby plankton said. "I've got my basket ready to go!"

Sheriff Shrimp gave the little baby plankton a pat on the shoulder. "That's great. You have fun now, y'hear?"

The baby plankton nodded and skipped off. Sheriff Shrimp tipped his hat once more at the parents. "Ma'am, sir. You have yourselves a terrific day now, y'hear?"

The plankton nodded and joined their daughter as they started walking toward the town square. Sheriff Shrimp looked on in admiration. This is why he did what he did. To meet people like this and learn a little more about their lives.

At the next two houses, he had similar encounters. Sheriff Shrimp met a lovely family of clownfish at the first home. They were having a family reunion, so one hundred and thirty-eight fish were squeezed into a small arrangement of wood. Sheriff Shrimp said hello to each fish individually. At the second of the two homes, Sheriff Shrimp helped extricate a puffer fish who had huffed and puffed a size too big and was trying to remove itself from the bathtub it had become stuck in. With Sheriff Shrimp's assistance, the fish was able to return to its weekend chores.

Sheriff Shrimp waved goodbye to the thankful fish and headed on down toward the final house in the row—the last home yet to be visited in all of his time as sheriff. He had shaken hands with everyone else in Scampi Bay, and he was very excited to meet the inhabitants within.

Knocking his tail on the door, Sheriff Shrimp removed his hat. The peephole cover slid open; a pair of eyes peeked through. "Yeah?" the eyes said. "What do ya want?"

Sheriff Shrimp wasn't sure who the voice belonged to, so he couldn't use his typical "ma'am" or "sir" introduction with a tip of his hat. Stammering ever so slightly, he said, "Well, hello there. I'm Sheriff Shrimp, the sheriff of Scampi Bay. I was just making my way around the neighborhood and wanted to say hello to all of the town-screatures. I realized I had never come up this way, and, well, it would be nice to meet you all."

Sheriff Shrimp added a smile at the end of his little introduction. He thought that improvisation went quite well! The peephole cover slammed shut. After a moment, the door opened.

A burly, mustachioed salmon emerged, closing the door behind him. "Now lookee here," the salmon said. "I ain't done nothin' wrong. Nothin' illegal. I'm a law-abidin' citizen, just like the rest of ya. So I don't want no trouble."

Sheriff Shrimp was taken aback. "Oh no, sir. I'm not bringing any trouble. Just coming by to say hello."

The salmon snorted. "You think I believe that? I seen your type coming round here before. Ya walk in all high and mighty and act like you can just come in and take over. Well I got news for ya, bub. Ya can't. This is my home and I won't have it."

Sheriff Shrimp scratched his antennae. He wasn't sure how to handle a situation like this. Everyone was usually so welcoming. "Well, sir, if I may . . . I don't know who you've met in the past, and I'm real sorry if they haven't treated you kindly, but I'm not like that. I have no ulterior motive, no hidden agenda, nothing like that. I simply want to meet you and shake your hand. That's not asking for too much, is it?"

The salmon peered down at Sheriff Shrimp. He still had a suspicious look in his eyes, though it softened slightly. "Just a handshake, ya say? Can tell a lot about a man by his handshake, that's for sure."

"I've been told I have a firm one," Sheriff Shrimp said, chuckling a bit too loudly at his own comment. "Though I bet you've got a solid grip, too."

"I reckon I do," the salmon said, nodding his head. "Had some good practice arm wrasslin' back in high school."

"Where did you go to high school, if I may ask?" Sheriff Shrimp said.

"Jumbo Coconut High," the salmon said. There was the smallest hint of pride in his voice. "Arm wrassled, did discus, and was a swimmer. Specialized in the hundred meters upstream. Played me some sports all year round. Varsity athlete in all of 'em, too."

"You might not believe this," Sheriff Shrimp said, "but I went to Jumbo Coconut High, too. Never was able to make the swim team but loved going to the meets."

"Now you're talkin'," the salmon said. "You know, you was right. You ain't like the others." He extended a fin. "Name's Sal. Put 'er there."

Just as Sheriff Shrimp reached up to shake with his new friend Sal, a darkness came over Scampi Bay. Sal and Sheriff Shrimp looked up. A big, brown mass was plummeting downward through the water.

"Jump!" Sheriff Shrimp yelled, diving off to his left. The object, whatever it was, crashed down next to him, sending dust flying everywhere. It made a horrible crunching sound as it landed. Sheriff Shrimp closed his eyes and covered his ears to try and dull the noise.

After a few moments, he couldn't hear anything at all. He unplugged his ears and saw more movement in the water. The brown mass was starting to retreat back upward in the water.

Sheriff Shrimp had seen fishermen's nets before, the ones that were attached to the ends of sticks. But this wasn't an ordinary fishing net. This net was larger than any he had ever come across. It looked to be nearly half the size of the ocean. It had been cast down into the water, consuming all of Scampi Bay.

Sheriff Shrimp took his hat off his head and held it somberly, watching as his entire town lifted toward the surface. At that moment, he'd give anything to be with them. But he was left alone to rebuild the pieces of the once proud Scampi Bay, now reduced to nothing in one fell swoop.

The Coffee Café

"OKAY, SO YOU WANT A DOUBLE CARAMEL MACCHIATO RAINBOW sprinkle special with half-and-half, a splash of skim milk, two sugars, one Splenda, and a dash of cinnamon?"

"No, you stupid idiot. One sugar and two Splendas. Were you even listening to a word I was saying?"

"Oh, yes. Sorry, sir."

The morning rush was winding down, and my last customer appeared to be running late for work. Sadly, this was one of the kinder interactions I've had at The Coffee Café, a little shop on Guerrero Street, just down the road from the hospital. I'd been working here for about a year, and I had seen how terrible humans could be, particularly when they haven't yet had their coffee.

"I swear, if there are two fucking sugars in this drink, I'm not paying for it." I glanced up at the man. He was wearing a crumpled suit that was maybe just an inch too short for him. Not only were the sleeves of his dress shirt extended too far out, his tie looked wound so tight that it was a wonder he hadn't passed out from suffocation. He had a messenger bag slung over his shoulder, with a smattering of papers poking out from the different compartments. I wondered if he had recently collided with a bus, as his haggard appearance suggested.

"No, sir," I said. "There will only be one fucking sugar."

"Don't you dare get smart with me," he said, a vein on his fore-head bulging out with every other word. "I make and break little shits like you every day."

"Sounds painful," I said, taking his credit card. "Would you like to donate any money to the . . . You know what? You seem like the kind of guy who wouldn't. I won't even bother asking."

"Good intuition," he said. "How long until my drink is ready?"

"That depends," I said as I handed the card back to him. "When are you going to stop yelling?"

"Just bring me my fucking drink."

I walked to the back of the store. It had already been a chaotic morning. Much like this customer, everyone seemed extra tense, and I hadn't been spared from the vitriol. Luckily, I'd get to relax as soon as this last, pleasant customer left. I briefly flirted with the idea of dumping two sugars into his drink, but I figured life was tough enough for him. He was already ticked off, and it wasn't even lunch-time yet.

Our caramel dispenser machine was the most difficult thing in the world to operate. Seeing someone slamming both hands on the pump, like they were giving CPR, wasn't uncommon. I had to smash it extra hard for this drink, the gooey buildup from previous orders not helping matters.

It's particularly rare for anyone to order a drink with sprinkles, es-pecially an adult. I always enjoyed when someone did, though, because our sprinkle shaker was fantastic. It was like playing the maracas. I gy-rated it intensely, my wrists loose, adding a little flair with my hips if the mood struck me. After the struggles with the caramel machine, this was a welcome treat. It was also the final touch on the order, so I was glad to be doing it. I could finally be done with this transaction.

"All right, sir, here you go," I said, placing a lid on top of the cup and sliding it before him. "One double caramel macchiato rainbow sprinkle special with half and half, a splash of skim milk, two Splendas, one sugar, and a dash of cinnamon. Literally going to be the best thing you taste all day."

"We'll see about that," he said, snatching the cup away like a hungry vulture.

He took a handful of napkins from the dispenser. That one I'll chalk up to poor design. People regularly came up to the counter just to grab a single napkin and would walk away with enough paper to mop up an entire puddle. Then the person, embarrassed by how many napkins were now in their possession, would shake their head, smile uncomfortably, and try to discreetly slide the napkins back in the dispenser. If I caught their eye while they were doing that, their grin got even wider. It was as if they had been caught doing something illegal and figured if they smiled long and hard enough, I wouldn't turn them in. As long as they didn't throw the napkins on the floor, I was totally fine with it.

The man lifted the lid off and took a sniff. "This smells like shit," he said. "Are you sure you got the order right?"

I pursed my lips, presenting the image of someone who cared deeply about this situation. I even uttered a "hmm" as I thought back to mere moments ago when I put together this order exactly as he had requested it.

"I most certainly did, sir." I said, after a few tense seconds had passed. "Sometimes when certain ingredients are mixed together, they can produce a . . . questionable odor, but rest assured, everything you've asked for is in there."

"I've ordered this before, and it doesn't smell this way," he said, sneering at me like I was a rodent on his front lawn. "You can pick out the individual ingredients without any problems. It shouldn't smell like this."

"I don't know what to tell you," I said. "I put all of your ingredients together. Maybe you're smelling somebody else's drink."

There was nobody else in the place. He was certainly smelling his own drink, but I had no idea why it wouldn't be aromatic. After all, with a handful of generally nice-smelling ingredients thrown in one cup, it should have at least been mildly pleasing to the nostrils.

He took a small sip, his face crinkling as he did so. "At least it *tastes* all right. Thanks." He clamped the lid back on and glared at me as he headed toward the door.

"Thanks for stopping at The Coffee Café," I called out to him. "Enjoy the rest of your day!"

He laughed. "Now that I'm out of here, I sure will." With that, he slammed the door.

Aside from the reverberating echo of the metal against the door-frame, The Coffee Café now stood silent. Normally, we had music playing, but I was the first employee to arrive and hadn't bothered turning any on. My mind is clearer when there isn't a Top Forty hit blasting in the background. And the only other worker who had come in, Loren, looked so hungover that I thought he might actually break like fine china if any sudden noises occurred. He had been sitting in the back room for more than an hour, trying to get his wits about him. Fortunately, business had been slow. I guess that was unfortunate for the business, but I sure didn't mind it. I was getting the same measly paycheck either way.

Noticing some scraps at a few tables, I grabbed a rag and hopped out from behind the counter. It never ceases to amaze me how people can be so messy. I understand maybe leaving a stirrer or a sugar packet or something small on the table, but I found two lids, a half-eaten sandwich, a nail file, a book entitled *Make Yourself Better Today: Stop Being Forgetful*, and what appeared to be a jar of olive oil, though there was no label on it. Certainly an odd mix of things to find at a coffee shop. Then again, we have an odd clientele.

I tossed the book back behind the counter and finished wiping down the tables. Nearly spotless! People never complimented the place for being clean and inviting, but I took a small joy in keeping things afloat. It was like I was battling an army of germs, and each newly washed table was a badge of honor. Or maybe I simply hadn't gotten enough sleep last night.

As I was gazing with pride at a particularly scrubbed-down slab of wood, Loren came out from the back room. "Dude," he said, his face contorted, "I just came out here to take a swig of milk. Good hangover cure, you know? And it is *rancid*. When's the expiration date on this thing?"

I squinted at him. "I don't know, Loren," I said. "You have the carton in your hand. Maybe take a look under your index finger?"

Loren shook his head and smiled. The light bulb had gone off. He lifted up his hand to reveal the date. "It says October seventh."

October? We were coming up on Thanksgiving. After all, nearly half our menu had some form of pumpkin in it. "Let me smell that real quick," I said, reaching for the carton.

Loren paused. "Okay, but don't hog it for too long," he said. "It's starting to make me more alert." He puffed his chest out, ready to attack the day with a fervor wielded by few men before him.

"You'll have it right back, don't worry." I had barely brought the milk up to my nose before I turned away. Loren was right; that was a *stench*. I suppressed a gag and handed it back to him. Maybe that's why the coffee I had made smelled so bad to that jerk. "Man, we gotta get rid of that milk."

"Not so fast!" he said. "Let me get a few more whiffs in." I've heard of sniffing glue; this was the first time I'd seen someone actually look forward to inhaling rancid milk. It was disgusting, but I admired Loren's persistence.

The door opened, and the little overhead bell rang. Plenty of places have some sort of indication to let you know there's a customer walking in, though The Coffee Café took it to another level. Rather than just a ding, *our* bell played a short five-second clip of chimes performing "Winter Wonderland." This was every day, regardless of the season. The bell had been installed last year around the holidays, and while it had gotten annoying after the third time I heard it, at least it made sense.

But the guy who had installed it left four days before Christmas, and nobody else knew how to undo the wiring to silence the chimes. So, we heard "Winter Wonderland" every day, even in the middle of a sweltering heat wave. People thought it was kitschy at first—our little way of saying, "It's hot outside, so why not have some fun with it?" I'm sure by now everyone knows we just can't figure out how to fix the door.

A beautiful brunette walked in. She was wearing a scarf tied in the most delicate way around her neck and a pea coat that radiated comfort. She walked with an air of confidence, her long legs reminiscent of a graceful gazelle stride. Her high heels lightly clicked on our linoleum floor, and her bright green eyes looked up at our menu board with anticipation. She came up to the counter and smiled, flashing a set of teeth so straight and perfect I nearly melted.

"Good morning," she said cheerfully. "I'll have a small coffee with just a hint of skim milk, please."

"You got it," I said. I imagined myself looking extremely suave as I casually leaned on the counter and took her cash. In my smoothest voice, I asked her the best question I could think of. "How's your morning going?"

"I start a new job today, right around the corner. I'm very excited!" she said. "I figured I'd come in and try out a cup of coffee. Who knows? Maybe this will be my new favorite spot! I already liked your little doorbell chime." She smiled again, and I nearly lost it. That smile could brighten up a black hole.

"We'd certainly enjoy that," I said as Loren began preparing her order. "What's the new job?"

"I'd rather not make any small talk, if that's okay," she said. She smiled once more, but this time seemed a bit more forced. "I had to do so much of it throughout the day at my last job, you know? Meetings, calls, even people in my apartment building—it's just so much. I appreciate you making my coffee, though."

"Oh, of course," I said. "Your order will be right out."

I stared glumly out at the tables while Loren finished making her drink. I noticed I had missed a spot.

"Alrighty, good to go!" Loren said. "Have a great first day at the new job."

"Thanks so much!" the woman said. "I'm starting as a senior data scientist for an aerospace company. I'll be tracking some of the most important spacecraft in the world, but we'll also be working on improving the automotive world, too. Things like optimizing traffic light patterns, understanding driving behaviors, and offering a more accurate view of rush hour by time and what kind of road you're on. My goal is to make it easier for you to get to and from work or anywhere, really."

"Hey, that's super neat!" Loren said. "Can't wait to hear all about it next time you stop in."

"I can't either," the woman said, flashing her smile as she headed out.

"I don't get it, man," I said. "I thought she said she didn't want to make small talk."

"I don't know," Loren said. "I just told her to have a good day. Sounds like a super cool job though. Not really for me. You know I'm no good at numbers. But she's getting to work on things that can make a difference."

He took another whiff of the rancid milk.

"Wait a minute," I said, a dread rising in my stomach. "You didn't use that for her order, did you?"

Loren's face froze. "Aw, man, I forgot she wanted milk!"

The Guy Who Was a Real Dud at Parties

ONCE, THERE WAS A GUY WHO WAS A REAL DUD AT PARTIES. HIS office would hold monthly events, things like happy hours or game nights. He'd always turn up even though the rest of the office could do without him. But they had to invite him by default since he worked there. And he often overheard their party-planning conversations anyway, so it would be rude to exclude him.

This latest party was going to be at a coworker's wife's best friend's house. She had dubbed it a "pre-Halloween party," which was her way of living out a midlife crisis even though she was only twenty-seven.

"It'll be a lot of fun!" she wrote in the invite, which she sent both through Facebook and snail mail. "Come dressed up as your favorite movie or book character."

The Guy Who Was a Real Dud at Parties had no intention of dressing up for the party. He overheard a coworker talking about *his* costume with another coworker, though they quickly halted the conversation when they noticed him by the sink peering at them.

"Hey, man," one coworker said. "How's it going?"

The Guy Who Was a Real Dud at Parties nodded and walked away.

THE PARTY WAS DUE to start at 9:30. Parties never start at a reasonable time anymore. And you never want to be the first one to a party, so no one actually shows up until a half hour later, at least. The Guy Who Was a Real Dud at Parties arrived at precisely 11:06. He was the fourteenth guest to enter and the first who wasn't in costume.

"Hi there!" a cheery voice greeted him. It was the coworker's wife's best friend. The two had never met before. "Welcome to the party. May I ask who you're dressed as?"

"Oh, I didn't come dressed as anyone," The Guy Who Was a Real Dud at Parties replied. "I don't have any costumes."

The host frowned for a second. "Maybe you're just a normal guy character. There are lots of those."

"No," said The Guy Who Was a Real Dud at Parties. "I'm not anybody else. I'm just here as myself." And with that, The Guy Who Was a Real Dud at Parties walked away.

IN THE LIVING ROOM, a group of four had gathered around a coffee table. As is the case at many parties, people are too timid to sit, or they feel it's rude to dirty up a couch and will often stand in a small circle to chitchat. But parties are precisely the reason anyone owns a couch. The host wants you to sit on the couch. Move the decorative throw pillows around. Spill the red wine on the cream cushions. Please, just *use* the couch.

Still, these people had not yet paired their bottoms with the couch. The Guy Who Was a Real Dud at Parties took the first step. He sat down and looked up at a man who was speaking. He was discussing something or other about politics.

"Have you ever run for office?" The Guy Who Was a Real Dud at Parties said, interrupting.

"I'm sorry," the man said. "Who are you?"

"Never mind that. Have you ever entered into a public race for office?"

"No, but I—"

"Then you're not really qualified to critique a politician's stance on something, are you?"

"I'm not sure I follow. We were just debating—"

"It's hardly a debate when it's simply you spouting off on topics you disagree with," The Guy Who Was a Real Dud at Parties said, "and quite frankly, on topics you don't understand."

"Oh, I don't understand them, huh?" The other man was getting flustered. The other man looked around at the others in the circle, scoffing to no one in particular. He put his drink down on the table but continued standing. "Mind enlightening me?"

"No, I'm trying not to spend the rest of my life at this party. Lovely as it is."

And with that, The Guy Who Was a Real Dud at Parties got up and walked away.

IN THE KITCHEN, a small group of women were eyeing the countertop. There were no fewer than five different kinds of chips, all displayed prominently in five brightly colored bowls. One woman separated herself from the group and went to grab a chip.

As she placed her hand in the bowl, another hand quickly moved on top of hers. She turned and looked into the eyes of the man whose hand was still touching hers.

"Well, this is quite the handshake," she cooed, giggling uncontrollably, and took a sip from the vodka and soda in her other hand.

The Guy Who Was a Real Dud at Parties smiled, though it

looked more like an uncomfortable sneer than a true smile. "I was just trying to get a chip," he said.

"Well, you got me instead!" She snorted and continued to giggle.

The Guy Who Was a Real Dud at Parties cringed. "Do you always laugh this much?"

"Only if a funny guy like yourself comes along." She had taken her hand out of the bowl and run her fingers up his arm. When she said "yourself," she gave him a little poke in the chest.

"I don't see how there's something funny about chips," The Guy Who Was a Real Dud at Parties said. "Sustenance is important, after all."

The girl stared at The Guy Who Was a Real Dud at Parties. "Oh my God! I was just thinking the same thing. That's why I came over here to have some—*hiccup*—chips!" Her words were starting to slur together. "And then I meet a man who's also trying to get a chip. Don't you think it's a little bit of fate?"

The Guy Who Was a Real Dud at Parties turned his head, trying to figure her out. "No. I think we both just wanted the same kind of chip."

"No, no, no!" She was almost hysterical now. She was clutching his shirt in her hands. With each word, she gave it a little tug. "This is fate! We were destined to meet and bond over chips."

"You know, I think you might be a little intoxicated."

"Are you meaning to tell me you don't—*hiccup*—drink?"

"I mean to tell you that when I do drink, I can control myself," The Guy Who Was a Real Dud at Parties said. "Unfortunately, it looks like you don't share that same sense of willpower."

"Why do you say that? Because I like to have a good time?" She was starting to dance with him now, pressing her body against his.

"I just worry that if I move, you'll fall down. You need to be more sensible."

She looked up, scowling. "Look! I didn't come to this party to be yelled at. You sound like my dad!" After that declaration, the woman stormed off. The rest of her friends watched her leave, then turned their attention back toward him.

"By the way," he said, leaning slightly toward them, "your costumes are dreadful." And with that, The Guy Who Was a Real Dud at Parties walked away.

WAITING FOR THE BATHROOM, The Guy Who Was a Real Dud at Parties found himself in line with another man, who was dressed as Clint Eastwood from the movie *Gran Torino*. The other man tried to make some small talk. "Some party, huh?" he said.

The Guy Who Was a Real Dud at Parties stared blankly at him. "Why are your pants up so high?"

The other man laughed. "I'm Clint Eastwood from *Gran Torino*."

"Clint Eastwood doesn't laugh. Not in *Gran Torino*. Not in *Dirty Harry*. Not in *Million Dollar Baby*. He just doesn't do it."

The other man looked confused. "Yeah, but . . . I'm not actually him. I just dressed like him."

"You're wearing a pair of sweatpants pulled incredibly high up, with your T-shirt tucked into them," The Guy Who Was a Real Dud at Parties said. "That's not really dressing like him. I'm not sure I could tell you apart from, say, an unemployed lard-ass sitting on his couch."

The other man had a concerned look on his face. "Come on, man, it's just a party. A fun time for us to dress up."

"But you're not putting any effort into it," The Guy Who Was a Real Dud at Parties said. "That's my point. Maybe if you dyed your hair white, or made your voice all gravelly, or spoke with extremely racist undertones . . . then I'd believe you were Clint Eastwood from *Gran Torino*. For now, you're just some lard-ass who's waiting in line for the bathroom."

"That's pretty rude."

"Then I guess it's rude to be honest," The Guy Who Was a Real Dud at Parties said. "Oh, look, it's Carlton from *The Fresh Prince.*"

Another man had joined the pair in line. He wore a striped long-sleeve shirt and khaki pants and was bopping his head all over the place. It seemed like he was listening to music that only he could hear. He drummed on his thighs as he joined the line.

"What? No. I'm Steve from *Blue's Clues,*" he said. "You know, that show on Nickelodeon from way back when? Like 'do you see a clue?' and it's right there behind him or under his nose? You'd have to be a real dummy not to spot the clue. I thought this getup was obvious!"

The Guy Who Was a Real Dud at Parties shrugged. "What can I say? You thought wrong. Your costume is pedestrian, at best. I will say you're better than Clint Eastwood over here."

"Ohhh, is that who you are?" Steve said. "I thought you were like old John Travolta from *Saturday Night Fever.*"

The man dressed as Clint Eastwood looked chagrined. "Nope," he said sullenly. "I'm Clint Eastwood."

"You just better hope the actual Clint Eastwood doesn't come to this party, or then we'll be in real trouble." And with that, The Guy Who Was a Real Dud at Parties walked into the bathroom.

"I HOPE YOU HAD A GOOD TIME!" the host said, as people started filing out the door. "Thank you so much for coming."

The Guy Who Was a Real Dud at Parties headed toward the exit. He extended a hand out to the host. "I can't say this party impressed me," he said. "Perhaps I set the bar too high."

The host shrugged. "I suppose you can't please everyone. It seemed like the rest of the party really enjoyed themselves."

"Well," The Guy Who Was a Real Dud at Parties said as he grabbed his coat from the closet, "the rest of the party also seemed to be full of dolts."

"Did you even come here with anyone?" the host asked. "Were you a plus-one?"

"I heard the invitation," The Guy Who Was a Real Dud at Parties said, stepping into the doorway. "So that was enough for me to attend. I thought this might really be something special."

"Hey, everyone else did think so," the host said. "I'll take that over pleasing you any day." The host slammed the door. The Guy Who Was a Real Dud at Parties sighed.

"Why do I never have a good time at any of these parties?" he asked the doorframe. After a minute, The Guy Who Was a Real Dud at Parties trudged away.

Walk of Fame

"YOU FOUND ME!" BRETT SAID, LAUGHING. "WAY TO GO."

Brett gave the little boy, who couldn't have been more than six or seven years old, a high five with his big white glove. The little boy smiled and ran off to his parents, who were wearing Mickey Mouse ears.

The parents approached Brett. "How much, Waldo?" the father asked.

Brett smiled. "Oh, it's nothing. He's just playing around."

"I appreciate that," the father said. "Here's a little something for your trouble, anyway."

The father handed Brett a crumpled bill, and the family was on their way. Brett unwrinkled it as they walked off. It was a two-dollar bill. Sadly, that was his best haul of the day so far. He put the bill in his pocket.

Brett had been a character actor for nearly six years. Waldo was a little tougher than some of the major superheroes. Kids didn't really experience Waldo much these days, and a new book hadn't come out in quite some time.

Still, he loved it. Getting to hide among the hustle and bustle of the Walk of Fame, interacting with people from all paths of life. Best of all, the costume required almost no maintenance whatsoever. Just a striped red and white shirt, a hat of similar colors, white gloves, glasses, and a pair of jeans. Brett had been around long enough to see some of the other performers go for more ambitious outfits. And he was thankful every day he didn't have to wear pounds of makeup or speak in an accent or don a heavy costume. In the winter, sure, you could be Iron Man or Chewbacca, but once June hit? Only the toughest survived.

Waldo had recently moved to a little space of sidewalk about three hundred feet long. His area started right around the star for the TV show *Rugrats*. Brett quite liked that show. He related all too well to the episode where Angelica became addicted to cookies.

The other performers on the block included Wonder Woman and Nightcrawler from *X-Men*. Within the past week they had been joined by Groot, the enormous, hulking tree creature who gained tremendous popularity after the *Guardians of the Galaxy* movie franchise launched. The detail on this costume was incredible, and Brett wondered how long it took to put together.

"Hey, Groot." Brett walked over to the creature. Even though this was someone in costume, he was still an impressive specimen, towering over Brett. Groot looked down at him.

"I am Groot," he said in a Yoda-esque voice, which was pretty much all Groot says in the movie and comic books. Something about a stiff larynx.

"Okay, you can drop the act," Brett said.

"I am Groot?" The inflection changed, but the script did not.

Brett sighed. "Look, all I want to know is how long it takes you to get ready in the morning."

"I am Groot!" the beast roared. Brett looked back blankly, and Groot held up three fingers.

"Three? Like, three *hours*?" Brett asked.

Groot nodded solemnly.

"Wow, that's amazing. Welcome to the block! Give me—uh, I mean, give Wonder Woman over there a shout if you ever need anything." He never liked Wonder Woman. She just seemed so arrogant and hardheaded. She deserved the irritation that came with trying to interact with Groot.

Groot's lips curled back in an attempt to smile. Brett backpedaled slowly, returning to his position.

"Waldo!" Brett turned to see two high school girls running toward him. They were followed by a man holding a camera, who looked very overwhelmed by everything happening around him.

"Hurry up, Dad!" one of the girls shouted. "We need to get a picture with Waldo!"

"Okay, honey," the man said. His sunglasses sat perched on his nose, the slightest bit crooked. He was wearing a Minnesota Twins baseball cap and, like many tourist dads, had his polo shirt tucked into his cargo shorts. Those shorts were pulled up about four inches too high. He steadied the camera at Waldo and the two girls. "One . . . two . . . and . . . three."

The camera took at least six photos. Each one felt like a dagger to the eyes. Even in the daylight, the flash was unbearable. Brett couldn't stop blinking, trying to stop the bright lights from invading his pupils.

"Thanks, Waldo!" the girls screamed. One of them leaned over and gave him a kiss on the cheek. They giggled and ran on down the block.

"Now hold on, girls!" the father yelled after them.

"Don't worry, Dad!" one shouted back. "We won't be going far!" They darted out of sight.

"So . . . do I pay you for this?" the man asked.

Brett opened his mouth to respond. Normally he was more relaxed about payment, but today was extra slow. It was time to take a chance. "Yes," he said. "Twenty dollars for a photo, plus tip."

"Oh," the man said, "that's not a bad deal! Here's your twenty, and here's a little extra." The man handed Brett two crisp twenty-dollar bills. Brett tried to hide his excitement.

"Thank you, sir!" he said, grinning and waving. "Enjoy the rest of your stay in California."

"Thank *you*, Waldo. Oh, did you see which way my girls went?"

Brett pointed down the street. He knew exactly where they were. He could still hear their laughter. The man scampered off, waving over his head.

Brett carefully placed the bills in his wallet. It was rare enough to even make ten dollars in a single transaction, let alone double that, plus tip.

He thought about lunch. He could actually splurge. Maybe he'd visit Isabel's, the steakhouse a few blocks south. He passed it on his walk from the bus stop but had never actually gone inside. Today would be the day.

Brett made another eight dollars from pictures over the next half hour. He checked his watch after saying goodbye to a pair of five-year-old twins visiting from Bolivia. His Spanish wasn't great, but he had survived the conversation. The watch read 12:57. Brett figured it was a good time to go grab a bite to eat.

He wandered down the block to where Nightcrawler was shaking hands with a frail-looking elderly woman. He had a strong, intense presence but could also turn on the charm like a faucet. Brett admired that switch, though he found himself a little scared around Nightcrawler. In fact, Nightcrawler had been so intimidating the first couple of times the duo met that Brett hadn't learned the actor's actual name. Now it seemed too far into the relationship to ask.

"So wonderful to meet you," Nightcrawler said, as the old woman walked away.

Brett smiled at the woman, then turned to Nightcrawler. "Hey, you eat yet?"

"Nah, was just thinking about taking lunch."

"Cool. Wanna check out Isabel's?" Brett was feeling confident from his haul thus far. "I'm really craving a steak."

"Actually, yeah, that sounds great," Nightcrawler said. "I've done well today, so I think I deserve a little splurge."

"Oh yeah?" Brett said. "How much? If you don't mind me asking, of course."

"Close to eight hundred dollars so far. People are tipping like crazy today. Isn't it great?"

Brett froze, a glaze coming over his eyes. "Yes . . . it's terrific."

"Right on. Let's meet back out here in fifteen? I gotta get out of this costume. It's hot out here."

"I HEAR THIS PLACE is so good, man," Nightcrawler said. "I'm excited to try it out. Thanks for inviting me."

"Yeah, my pleasure," Brett said, still in a daze. "Do you . . . do you make like eight hundred dollars every day?"

"Don't be ridiculous," Nightcrawler said as they sat down at a table. "It's maybe six hundred, if that. Usually about four or five. People are just being extra generous today. It's Friday, after all. And you know how people get on the weekend."

"Yeah," Brett replied weakly. "They don't . . . they don't seem to care about money on the weekends."

"Absolutely not," Nightcrawler said. "You know what sounds amazing? A top sirloin."

"That does sound good. Is it on the menu?"

"Wouldn't be much of a steakhouse without it!" Nightcrawler said. "Here it is. Fifty-six dollars. That's a little steep, but man, we've earned it. And you get a baked potato, too."

Brett's heart sank. He had only earned fifty-five dollars today. "You know, I'm not really that hungry. Maybe I'll go for something a little less filling. This salad looks good."

"Nonsense," Nightcrawler said. "Sirloins for both of us. Let's split a bottle of wine, too. It'll make the afternoon a whole lot more interesting!"

"Uh, okay," Brett managed to spit out. How in the world was he going to pull this off?

Their server came over to their table—a chipper young woman wearing a big smile.

"Hey there!" she said. "My name is Laura, and I'll be your server today. Would you two like anything to drink?"

"I'll have a water," Brett said. "Just a water."

Nightcrawler laughed. "Waters for both of us, and then we'll split a bottle of this 1979 Syrah you have."

"Excellent!" Laura said, seemingly unaware of Brett's growing desperation. "I'll have that right out. Did you need a few more minutes to look over the menu?"

"Nope, I think we're both going with the sirloin," Nightcrawler said, looking over at Brett. There was just the slightest hint of malice in his eyes. Brett knew anything besides the sirloin would be unacceptable.

"Yes," Brett said, managing a smile. "Yes. That."

"Wonderful!" Laura chirped. "How would you like it cooked?"

"Medium rare, of course," Nightcrawler bellowed. "Is there any other way to enjoy a steak?"

Brett preferred his well done, but he wasn't about to say anything to Nightcrawler. He nodded his head slightly.

"Perfect!" Laura said, her shrill voice almost at a shouting level. "We'll get those out to you ASAP!"

As she left, Nightcrawler leaned back in his chair. He was staring at Brett, a slight smirk on his face. He sat that way for three minutes, not uttering a word. Finally, Brett had to break the silence.

"Great weather out there, huh?" he asked.

"Don't jerk me around, man," Nightcrawler said. "First, you invite me out to steak. Then you get all wishy-washy. You didn't want wine; you were talking about a salad. What gives?"

"I just—" Brett couldn't admit to Nightcrawler that he had only made pennies today, compared to what Nightcrawler was raking in.

"You just what? Realized you couldn't afford this meal?"

Brett tilted his head. "How do you figure that?"

"For starters," Nightcrawler said, counting with his fingers, "since we've sat down, you've been looking around like you're planning to dine and dash. You also tried to order a salad, which is basically the cheapest thing on the menu. And I saw you check your wallet. You're not very discreet, you know."

Brett hung his head in shame. "I just thought I had made a decent amount of money today, and I wanted to celebrate."

"Celebrate, then!" Nightcrawler said. He leaned over to give Brett a hearty pat on the shoulder. Instead it was a hefty slap on the clavicle.

Brett rubbed his shoulder. "But this is even more expensive than I thought. I don't want to blow so much money here. In fact . . . I don't even *have* the money to blow here."

"What do you mean? How much have you made today?"

"I'd really prefer not to say . . ." Brett looked up toward the ceiling.

"Tell me. I want to know."

"I made less than this lunch is going to cost, okay? Especially with a bottle of Syrah. Do you even know what that is?" Brett was huffing by this point. He felt his face burning.

Nightcrawler leaned forward and grabbed Brett by the elbow. "You know why you haven't made anything?" Brett shook his head. "Because you're too *nice*. It's a dog-eat-dog world out there, man. Sure, you might have an old lady or two, or someone who throws you a buck here or there for being sweet, but the real money? That's from the rich saps who walk around Hollywood trying to impress their plastic wives or their spoiled kids. Or it's those same plastic wives who are taking a break from their idiotic husbands. And they want to meet someone cool. They don't want some nice guy who can hide. Look at me. I'm the coolest dude you know, right?"

Brett didn't necessarily agree with that but found himself nodding anyway.

"It's because I have the swagger you need to stay on top out there," Nightcrawler said. "There's a lot of money to go around, but you gotta shake the people up for it a little bit. Say some shit that's a little insulting. That's cool. You gotta be cool if you want to eat steak. I've seen you out there, my friend. You are not cool. You're too nice. That's why you're sitting here with rags in your pockets, instead of cash. Stop being nice and start getting paid."

Brett frowned. "So that's all I need to do? Be mean?"

Nightcrawler leaned forward even more. He was inches away from Brett's face. "Yes. Being mean exudes confidence. It's what makes people say, 'That guy knows what he's doing, and he's going to get what he wants.' You need to have that confidence to get anywhere in life. I tell you what. Practice with our server. When she comes back with the steaks, tell her yours isn't cooked to perfection, and you aren't going to accept anything less."

"But what if it's cooked how I like it?"

Nightcrawler shook his head and sighed. "That doesn't matter. The point is, you're a confident man who knows what he wants. And what is in front of him simply won't cut it. Just be a little snide to her, and she'll fix it. You'll see how good it feels."

"Okay, I'll give it a try," Brett said, in a very unconfident manner.

Laura returned with a bottle of wine. "I'm terribly sorry, gentlemen," she began. "But we only have a 1983 bottle of the Syrah you ordered. I hope that's okay."

Nightcrawler's eyes caught Brett's. He smirked and turned back to Laura. "Unfortunately, no. That will not be okay. We'd like to drink what we ordered, please."

Brett's stomach turned. He couldn't believe how Nightcrawler was acting. This wasn't any way to treat people. No way would this work. Just no way.

"Certainly, sir," Laura said, humbly bowing as she backed away. "I'll see what I can do."

Nightcrawler raised his water glass in the air. "And that's how it's done. Cheers, man."

Moments later, a man dressed in a full suit came up to the table. "Gentlemen," he said. "I apologize for our lack of wine. We certainly don't want anything on our menu that isn't readily available, so I've sent your server out to pick up a bottle of Syrah, aged since 1979. I hope you'll bear with us during this terrible inconvenience. Of course, the bottle will be on the house."

Nightcrawler looked disgusted as he stared the man down. After a long pause, he muttered, "I *guess* that's okay. I just hope you're better prepared next time."

"We most certainly will be, sir," the man in the suit said. "Thank you for your understanding. Your food and wine will be out shortly."

Nightcrawler nodded dismissively as the man left the table. Brett sat, his mouth agape. "I can't believe it," he mumbled. "I just can't believe it."

"I don't think it's hard to understand, man," Nightcrawler said. "You radiate confidence, good things come to you."

Several minutes later, Laura returned to the table, holding out the bottle of '79 Syrah. She poured the tiniest bit into Nightcrawler's glass. He swirled it around, stuck his nose into the glass, and took a sip. He turned to her, smiling. "It's perfect, thank you."

"Very good, sir," Laura said, filling each glass about halfway. "Your steaks will be out in a minute."

"See?" Nightcrawler said after Laura had left the table. "I was nice there, got her confidence built back up. Then you criticize the steaks to show you know what you want. You can do it." Nightcrawler clinked Brett's glass.

"You know what?" Nightcrawler said. "I don't even give a shit about wine. It all tastes the same to me. If she hadn't said anything, I never would have known that was something different from what I ordered. I can tell the difference between red and white, and that's about it. She just did herself in by admitting defeat. That's no way to impress someone."

Brett sipped on his wine. It tasted bitter. "I usually just stick with water," he said quietly.

"Not when you're with me," Nightcrawler bellowed. "We live it up! Now, when she comes back, what are you going to say?"

"That . . . that the steaks aren't cooked properly," Brett managed to squeak out.

"Very good," Nightcrawler said. "You can't bring that weak stuff to the table and get away with it."

Laura returned to the table, carrying a tray with two meaty steaks on it. She set down Nightcrawler's dish first, and then placed the other plate in front of Brett. The smell was intoxicating—the steak flanked on either side by vegetables and a baked potato. Brett was starving and almost began digging in. But Laura interrupted.

"Would you gentlemen mind cutting into your steaks and letting me know if they're cooked properly?" she asked.

Brett looked over at Nightcrawler, who was cocking an eyebrow. Brett grabbed his fork and knife and began sawing back and forth at the meat. It cut very easily, as it was cooked a perfect medium rare. Just like he ordered. He tried to silently convey as much to Nightcrawler, but his dining companion would have none of it. Brett looked up at Laura.

"Actually," he said. "I ordered medium rare, and this looks to be a bit more well done than that."

Laura smiled at him, then leaned forward. Brett thought she was grabbing his plate, but instead, she grabbed his collar. She yanked him down to the table, his eyes inches away from his steak.

"Take another look," she hissed. "Because that seems perfectly medium rare to me. Your dining partner may have the upper hand on me in terms of wines, but nobody, and I mean *nobody*, is going to tell me a steak isn't cooked properly if it is. Do you even know what medium rare is supposed to look like? Do you have a camera on you? Because you can take a picture of this steak in front of you and staple it to your eyelids so you remember forever and ever. That is cooked medium rare, and you're going to enjoy it. Matter of fact, if you so much as say one thing to me during this entire meal that isn't 'thank you' or 'goodbye,' I'm going to mash your face into this plate. And I couldn't care less who sees me. No more shit from you. Got it?"

She still had a death grip on Brett's collar, so he mustered the best nod he could. It sufficed; Laura threw him back in his chair.

"Well then," she said, a pleasant smile returning to her face. "Glad everything is to your satisfaction. Please let me know if you need anything, okay, gentlemen?"

She waltzed away, and Nightcrawler slammed the table. "Holy hell, man! I had her all wrong. That girl is fierce as shit. Did you see how she just put you in your place? That was amazing!"

Brett took a bite of his steak. It tasted like defeat.

BRETT TOOK HIS PLACE back on the Walk of Fame after Nightcrawler had chipped in a few extra dollars to help cover Brett's portion of the meal, saying he could pay him back once he grew a spine.

Brett walked by Groot, who was hugging a small boy with the

delicate touch of a comic book collector sealing a mint-condition issue in protective wrapping. While the boy was smiling from ear to ear, his dad slipped a crisp one-hundred-dollar bill into Groot's hand. "I am Groot," the hulking tree-man said humbly.

"Shut up, Groot," Brett muttered.

Just then, a family passed by. The father seemed incredibly out of his element, mouth agape as he took in everything around him. His wife couldn't have been more bored; she was looking around the block, searching for a way to escape the situation she found herself in. And the trio of kids in front of them certainly weren't helping matters. Brett had gotten pretty good at guessing ages, and he'd put these children squarely in the seven- to twelve-year-old range. Just young enough to still throw a tantrum and get away with it, but old enough to know how to wrestle what they wanted from their parents.

Brett thought back to what Nightcrawler had told him. This family seemed like the perfect target. "Hey, aren't you gonna take a picture with me?" The entire family turned toward Brett. The father smiled broadly, while the mother looked him up and down. She shrugged and nodded to herself, like she could do worse. The youngest kid walked up to him.

"Who the hell are you? A guy in a striped shirt?"

"Now, now, honey, that's Waldo," the father said. "He was a big part of my childhood growing up."

The man stuck his hand out to Brett to shake it.

"Now, that'd normally be fifty for the handshake," Brett began. "But I tell you what, since you're a big fan of mine, I'll knock off ten bucks. And if you get a photo package with the whole family, it's only a hundred, total."

"A hundred bucks?" The man took a step back from Brett. "I guess I'm already in the hole for a handshake, so why not? Can you lift up my kids, too?"

"Sure! They seem small enough." Brett immediately regretted agreeing to this. The kids did not look small at all. Why had he said that?

The children hesitantly walked over to Brett. They still didn't seem sure of who he was, but the father was Waldo's biggest supporter. He gave his camera to his wife. "All right, honey, let's try and get one where we're all looking this time."

The woman peered out from behind the camera lens. "Don't get sassy with me, Jeremy," she said. "It's hard enough to get these kids to sit still for a second, much less look at a camera lens. I don't have all day."

The man sighed and looked at Brett, then back at his kids. "All right, kiddos, up into the nice man's arms."

Working in tandem, the man and Brett somehow got a kid perched on his shoulders and one in each arm. The next few minutes were excruciating. The kid around his neck kept pulling on his ears, while the one in his right arm seemed to find great joy in kicking his leg. The one in his left arm was fairly well-behaved, but she was incredibly sticky. This was why Brett didn't like picking up children. They were always sticky.

"That's it, Jeremy, I'm done," the woman said. "Surely one of those is usable. Now pay this weirdo so we can get out of here."

"Who are you calling a weirdo?" Brett said. "That's mean."

"Obviously I'm calling you one, you weirdo," the woman said. "Now go back to hiding or whatever it is you're known for."

"Don't worry about her," her husband said, coming over to pay. "She's mad because we were supposed to go to Europe for a month but came here instead. Turns out my frequent flyer miles don't apply to international flights."

He handed Brett six twenty-dollar bills. It was the most he had ever made from a single interaction.

"You know something?" the man said. "We've walked along nearly this whole stretch, and you've been the nicest person out here. I really appreciate it. Nice to get a break from all the cruelty out there."

"Why, thank you!" Brett said. "Hope you all have a wonderful vacation. You'll get to Europe someday!"

"Yeah, we will!" the man replied. "Take care, now."

Brett smiled. Maybe being nice really could pay off. He would only have to be a little more assertive. That would be his new strategy. He didn't have to be mean like Nightcrawler said.

And next time, he'd get his steak done the way *he* wanted.

One More Hit

"NO, NO, *NO!*" EDWIN YANKED OFF HIS HEADPHONES. "THAT DOESN'T sound right at all!"

"Okay, Edwin," said Nick, the producer. "Why don't we take five?"

"Sure, I'll take five," Edwin grumbled. "I've been taking five for years."

In fact, it had been twenty-four years since "Crazy Lover," Edwin's debut hit, tore up the airwaves. You couldn't go anywhere without hearing it. It was on the radio, in commercials, in the background of movies, on bar jukeboxes, at amusement parks, and even parodied by songs like "Lazy Mother" and "Hazy Blunder."

Edwin earned a lot of money from "Crazy Lover," too, more than twenty million dollars. Of course, he had blown through most of it purchasing gifts for his family and friends. At the time, buying a trio of yachts didn't seem like a bad idea. Owning a dial-up modem repair service appeared to be a good investment back then. And the thirty-by-thirty-five-foot trampoline in the backyard? Well . . . that was still a lot of fun. He didn't regret that impulse buy at all.

But in the years since, he hadn't created anything that reached the success of "Crazy Lover." And it wasn't for lack of trying. He had released no fewer than sixteen singles over the past twenty-four years, and none of them had cracked the Hot 100 Billboard chart. He'd settle for making the top hundred of any genre and had dabbled in R&B, rock, and even rap in an attempt to chart once again. Boy, was *that* ever a mistake.

The rap song, entitled "Comin' Right Back Atcha," was a duo with MC Cemetery, released about seven years back. Edwin had provided the hook and the bridge and even tried his hand at rapping for eight bars. It was a disaster and made it onto every worst-song-of-the-year list. MC Cemetery actually retired from music after it came out. The last time Edwin had spoken with him, Cemetery was serving as the director of a funeral parlor. Seemed fitting.

Edwin wasn't deterred so easily. Sure, he took a twenty-month hiatus from all public appearances, and a lot of that time was spent deciding whether to stay in bed or get up and drag himself over to the couch. But once that hiatus was over, he was back in the studio, dropping his most recent album, *More Than a One-Trick Pony*.

That album was about as well-received as his rap song had been. Edwin tried to return to the pop world, but the twelve-song record got all kinds of negative reviews: "Edwin should have stuck with rapping." "I wouldn't wish this upon my worst enemies." "Just go ahead and apologize to your ears right now."

Those kinds of comments stung. Edwin was proud of what he achieved, but he just wanted one more big hit. Just one more ride to the top. . . .

"All right, Edwin." Nick had returned to the studio. "Let's get back to work."

THE SONG EDWIN WAS WORKING on was part of an EP he was putting together. Four songs with a live band. None of that synthetic stuff this time around. Edwin planned to release all four songs to radio stations over the course of the next year and let the listeners pick their favorites. One of them had to stick. That whole plan was dependent on track number one, though. He needed it to be perfect.

After laying down the verses and bridge, Edwin was struggling to deliver the chorus the way he wanted. It shouldn't be this hard, he thought. Four simple lines:

I was certain you were the one for me.
But you left, and now we're history.
In my mind, is where you're gonna be.
Your love will always make me crazy.

The "crazy" part was sung with six different harmonies, and Edwin wanted to provide them all. That'd be the word everyone could sing along with. Even if someone had never heard the song, it was accessible enough for the most tone-deaf of people to enjoy.

Edwin thought this song was clever, a sort of follow-up to "Crazy Lover." He shook his head and chuckled. Why had he never thought of this before? It made perfect sense—tap into an already established audience with the comeback hit and hopefully gain a few new listeners along the way.

"Why don't you try a falsetto?" Nick asked through the studio speaker.

Edwin nodded. Singing falsetto was one of his favorite things to do. Something about that high pitch seemed to make all of his cares disappear, if only for a moment.

As he dove into the "crazy," he knew this one was a winner. The falsetto pierced through the rest of the harmonies.

"How'd that sound in there?" he asked, though he already knew the answer.

Nick gave him a thumbs up.

"Damn right," Edwin mumbled. "This song is going to be a mega hit."

IT TOOK ANOTHER PAIR of eight-hour recording days for Edwin to finish up the chorus. The final time it came around, he added some howls and screams in the background. He was a fan of songs where the singer really showed some emotion. Especially since this song was about a jilted, crazed lover, it seemed appropriate. Then the very last note of his vocals would be nearly inaudible. The thunderous sounds all uniting into one final chime of heartbreak.

"Crazyyyyy," Edwin sang, his voice barely above a whisper. The final note of the song reverberated through his headphones. Cello, guitar, bass, crash cymbal—they all came together as one, along with the faint sound of Edwin's voice.

"Well, Edwin," Nick said through the loudspeaker, "I think that's a wrap."

Edwin could hear pride in Nick's statement. There's no better feeling in the world than completing a song. All of the garbage he had put out in the twenty-four years since "Crazy Lover" was well worth it. He was going to top the charts once again.

"Call the radio stations," Edwin said. "Tell them to make room in their rotations."

"Nice rhyme, Edwin!"

Edwin smirked. He wasn't even trying to rhyme.

"SORRY, EDWIN, IT'S JUST NOT resonating with the audience."

"What do you mean? It's a hit!" Edwin said. He was on the phone with a producer for the Sammy Slimeball Show, the top show on the number one station in the country. If Sammy Slimeball liked a song, there was no way it could fail.

"Your Love Makes Me Crazy" was marking four weeks since its release. And it wasn't soaring up the charts like Edwin had expected. Though by this point, Edwin would take a slow stumble up the charts.

"I mean, it seems like it has all the elements of a hit, sure," the producer replied. "But whenever we play it, there's simply no reaction. The board doesn't light up. We don't see anything on social media. Our email blast announcing it as your comeback didn't get any clicks. No one has even called in to request it. It's just . . . there, you know? But it's not moving the needle at all."

Edwin sank back in his chair. Maybe this was it. He'd poured his heart and soul into this latest project, and it was met with a resounding shrug of the shoulders.

"Look, don't feel too bad," the producer said. "Think about your last few albums. They've been terrible, to put it bluntly. I'm shocked you even wanted to get back into the music game. You've seen what happened with MC Cemetery, I'm sure. He quit the industry entirely."

"Yeah, I know all about Cemetery," Edwin said. "But we're not talking about him; we're talking about me."

"That's what I'm saying," the producer said. "You got such a backlash from those last albums that to hear crickets with this one is almost a relief, isn't it? People don't hate this one."

"No, that's even worse!" Edwin bellowed. "At least back then people were still talking about me. But if no one's calling in or requesting a song, it's like they've forgotten about me."

The voice on the other end of the phone was silent. Edwin sighed into the receiver.

"Anyway, we've gotta start the show," the producer said. "Good chatting with you, Edwin. Take care." There was a click and the call ended. Edwin held the receiver to his ear for a few more seconds before letting it fall into his lap.

"YOU JUST HEARD THE REMIX of 'Your Love Makes Me Crazy' making a huge jump! Up forty-seven spots to number four on our countdown. Next, we've got 'Reasonably Grounded Sex Life,' by The Shower Curtains."

Edwin turned off the radio. Another four months had passed since the Sammy Slimeball Show had told him his song wasn't cut out to be a hit. And that producer was right, in a sense. Edwin's song hadn't made a dent on the airwaves.

But Nick, Edwin's producer, didn't want to give up. He spent three months tinkering with "Your Love Makes Me Crazy," adding synthesizers, Auto-Tune, additional backup vocals, and an impressive sax solo toward the end of the song. The sax was synthetically played from a stock library of musical sound effects, but Nick was such a skilled producer he made it sound real.

The end result, the "Your Love Makes Me Crazy" remix, had taken the world by storm. It sold a million copies in its first twenty-four hours and had more streams in the first week than any song in history.

Edwin's phone rang. He picked it up without saying hello.

"Edwin, did you hear? You cracked the top five on the Sammy Slimeball Countdown Show!" Nick was ecstatic on the other end. "This is huge, man. Congrats!"

"You mean *you* cracked the top five," Edwin said. "It's your song now. It barely sounds like what I put together."

"What are you talking about?" Nick asked. "It's still your tune at heart. I only added a few bells and whistles to make it really pop. But it's nothing without you."

"Yeah, whatever you say," Edwin said. "Look, I've got to go. Congrats on the top five."

Edwin hung up the phone and fell onto his couch. He glanced over at the end table. There was a copy of his debut CD on it, the one that featured "Crazy Lover." He turned it over, studying the back cover. Looking at it now, it seemed so foreign, yet so familiar. He was wearing a leather coat and a white T-shirt, with faded jeans and old sneakers.

Edwin looked down. He was wearing a white T-shirt and faded jeans, with a different but still old pair of sneakers. He glanced at the table across the room. It had a leather jacket on it. Edwin laughed. He was the same guy he was twenty-four years ago. Desperate for fame, for accolades, for people telling him he was doing a good job.

He was getting that fame again. His name was back on everyone's lips. Yet this time, it was merely as a footnote. When people talked about the song, they'd mention him as the artist, but it was what Nick had done that really elevated the song into a hit. Nick was getting all the praise.

Edwin got up and walked over to his desk. He grabbed the CD player he kept there, the one he was using when "Crazy Lover" became a hit. Edwin placed his debut album inside the player and closed the lid. He put the headphones on, plopped back onto the couch, and pressed play. The opening chords of the first track hit his ears. Edwin closed his eyes and smiled.

Online Dating

"DUDE, YOU SHOULD TOTALLY PUT A PICTURE OF YOU HOLDING A kitten. Chicks *love* that stuff."

"Oh, come on, man. That's so corny."

"No, dude, trust me. Besides, you've got so many with your shirt off. They're going to think you're just a jock. You gotta show 'em your sensitive side, too."

"Fine. I think I have one on my desktop."

"Awesome, dude. And put that you like white wine and cuddling. You know the chicks are gonna eat that up."

"But I hate white wine—and cuddling just makes my arm fall asleep."

"Dude, think about it. You have to write this from their perspective. What would a chick like? Then you put it in. Kittens. Wine. Cuddling."

"Hmm, maybe you're right."

"Course I am, dude. Oh, and your favorite movie is *The Notebook*. Put it as your favorite book, too."

"I've never seen the movie. It looked stupid."

"Remember, dude. Think from *their* perspective."

"Oh, yeah. I'll type it in."

"It's going to work, dude. Trust me."

"THAT'S GROSS, JACKIE! Look at all the pictures he has without his shirt!"

"But he's holding a kitten in this one. He's *sensitive*."

"I guess you're right. That kitten does look really happy."

"See? And look! His favorite movie is *The Notebook*. You've seen that movie like a million times. It's his favorite book, too! Have you even read the book?"

"Wow. I didn't know there *was* a book."

"Maybe you two can read it together while you cuddle! Cuddling is one of his hobbies. He's such a sensitive guy!"

"Cuddling can be a hobby?"

"Of course! How many guys have you met that actually like cuddling?"

"I guess you're right, Jackie."

"Of course I'm right! And he enjoys sipping on white wine, too. You should ask him if he likes Chardonnay or Sauvignon Blanc."

"Okay, Jackie. If you think that'll work."

"Oh, it's going to work. Trust me."

"DUDE, YOU'VE BEEN MESSAGING back and forth for nearly two hours. Why don't you set up a date? Ask for her number, at least."

"Isn't that coming off as aggressive?"

"No, dude. It comes off as confidence. And chicks *love* confidence."

"Yeah, I think I've heard that before."

"Probably from me, dude. I know what I'm talking about."

"I just feel like we haven't said anything. Our first six messages were variations of 'hi' and 'hello.' And these past four have been us looking at each other's profile questions and commenting about them. Do I really care that she doesn't think a girl that's slept with a hundred people is a bad person, or that she thinks a right-handed glove turned inside out fits on her left hand? Why are these even questions on here?"

"Dude, don't worry about that. This is how it starts. You small talk, and then you invite her out for a drink. Even throw in dinner if you want."

"Dinner, too? That sounds kind of romantic."

"Oh, it absolutely is, dude. Chicks love that. A guy that can take care of them and show a little romance? You can't lose."

"I wonder what kind of food she likes. Maybe I'll ask her."

"No, dude. Confidence. Just pick a place and trust that she'll like it. Even if she doesn't, she'll appreciate that you made a decision. Chicks love guys that have direction in their lives."

"Oh, okay. If you think that'll work. Maybe Italian. That's romantic, right?"

"Totally, dude. Trust me, it'll work."

"WOW, CAMMELLO GOBBA? That place is fancy, fancy! And you *love* Italian food, too!"

"Yeah, I enjoy it every once in a while. Have you been there before, Jackie? Is it any good?"

"Have I been there? Of course not! That's one of the nicest places in town. You know I don't hang out with guys like that."

"That's true, Jackie. I wonder what I'm going to wear."

"It better be something magnificent! If he's inviting you to Cammello Gobba on your first date, he's definitely worth hanging on to."

"You think so? Maybe he just really likes Italian food or knows someone who works there."

"Even if he does, there are so many other cheaper options. Cafe Italiano . . . The Pasta Palace . . . Mamma Mia Eat Some Pizza . . . but no, he chose this one. He knows what he's doing."

"Maybe you're right, Jackie."

"Of course I'm right! Now, what to do about your outfit?"

"I have this blue dress I've only worn once. It's really nice!"

"I don't know if I've seen that one. Go put it on. Fashion show!"

"Okay, Jackie. I'll put it on. You can stop clapping now. You're so silly."

"I'm just excited—you might be meeting the one tonight! Look at this. You've answered nearly every question the same way. He also says a girl that's slept with a hundred guys isn't a bad person and turning a right-handed glove inside out means it'll fit on your left hand. There are so many different options for these. The fact he picked the same ones you did? That's incredible!"

"I didn't really pay much attention to those, Jackie. They only said I needed to answer four hundred questions to get the full benefits of the site."

"But deep down, this is how you really feel. It's your subconscious answering."

"If you say so, Jackie."

"I do—I know what I'm talking about. Now let's see that dress."

"I . . . I feel a little embarrassed in it, Jackie."

"Why, girl? You look *amazing*. It's not too short, so you're telling him you're classy. But you are giving off a hint of cleavage. That shows him you're very sexy, too."

"You're just saying that."

"No, I mean it! I actually want to borrow that dress myself."

"Let me go on the date first, Jackie!"

"Of course. But after that?"

"We'll see, Jackie. Stop clapping."

"IS THAT WHAT YOU'RE WEARING, DUDE?"

"Why, what's wrong with it?"

"Well . . . exactly what are you trying to achieve? You've got a couple rips in your jeans. Your shirt is halfway tucked in, with one side of the collar popped up. And your shoes—I wouldn't even wear those to a movie theater, let alone a fancy restaurant. Don't you have any nicer clothes, dude?"

"I mean, not really. Work is so casual; people show up in a T-shirt and shorts all the time. And most of my dates aren't this, you know, *glitzy.*"

"Every guy should have at least two classy outfits, dude. When's the date?"

"I'm picking her up at seven."

"And what time is it now?"

"You're wearing a watch."

"Yeah, but it's been broken for a couple of weeks. Just tell me what time it is, dude."

"Um . . . my phone's got 4:12."

"Perfect. Plenty of time to find you something for tonight. Grab your keys, dude. We're going shopping."

"Wait, what?"

"HE'S REALLY NOT PICKING YOU UP?"

"Oh, Jackie, times have changed. It's totally normal to meet at the restaurant."

"Did he give an excuse for why he can't get you?"

"Something about going shopping? I don't know. He sounded really rushed."

"How can you tell? Didn't he only send you a message?"

"Yes, Jackie. But I can tell from his words."

"What did he say?"

"Hold on, let me pull my phone out."

"This had better be good."

"He said, 'Hey! I'm so sorry to do this, but do you mind just meeting there? I had a snafu while shopping, and now I'm really rushed. But I'm looking forward to tonight!' See? I told you he was rushed, Jackie."

"Oh, you're a real Sherlock Holmes, all right."

"Either way, I think it's nice that he told me. So I'm not waiting for too long."

"If he's dressed half as nice as you are, maybe that shopping trip will have been worth it."

"Oh, stop it, Jackie. You're making me blush."

"I STILL DON'T KNOW WHY you had to come with me."

"Dude, trust me. I'm simply going to hang out by the bar and make sure everything's going smoothly. You'll hardly even know I'm here."

"No, I definitely know you're here."

"Look, dude, if you had any decent clothes, we wouldn't have had to go shopping, and I wouldn't have had to come with you on your date."

"Somehow I doubt that last part. I think you still would have shown up."

"Whatever, dude. You should be thankful I'm looking out for you."

"Come on. You know I appreciate the help. It's just . . . I don't really need you for this part, you know?"

"But you do, dude. You just don't know it."

"What are you even going to do, anyway? If the date isn't going smoothly, I mean."

"Don't worry about it, dude. I've got a plan."

"Do I get to hear anything about this plan?"

"Nah, dude. I don't want you to be preoccupied. I'll be at the bar over here. Go out there and have a good time. Be yourself."

"She thinks I'm somebody else, though. Most of the stuff I put in my profile you told me to add. Because chicks dig it, remember?"

"Those are slight embellishments we made, dude. She'll still like you for who you are deep down."

"Should I have watched *The Notebook* beforehand? What if she asks me about it?"

"Nah, dude. If she does, say that you want to talk about *her* instead, not about some movie."

"Wow . . . that's actually pretty good."

"Course it is, dude. I told you, you're gonna be glad I'm here."

"THANKS FOR THE RIDE, JACKIE. I really appreciate it."

"Of course, girl. I got your back. I'll be here the whole time in case things go south quickly."

"Oh, you don't have to do that, Jackie. I think I'll have a good enough time."

"You never know. Besides, if you don't like him and you have to bail, how would you get back home?"

"We only live six blocks away. I could walk, Jackie."

"In that dress? And those heels? Absolutely not. You'd have men catcalling you every step of the way! Or is that what you want?"

"I don't want that, Jackie. But I really think you're exaggerating. No man would notice."

"Let me tell you something about men. They notice. They notice *everything* about how a woman looks, as long as it stands out somehow. And you, girl, are standing out like crazy right now. In the best way possible, of course."

"Oh, come on, Jackie. You're only saying that to boost my confidence."

"No, I mean it! You're looking so hot tonight. He won't be able to turn you down. You'll be the one deciding if this date is a thumbs up or not."

"Gosh, Jackie. You really think I'll have that kind of power?"

"Absolutely! If you enjoy being with him, that's great. But if not, he won't stand a chance."

"Should we have some sort of signal if I'm not into him?"

"Just excuse yourself to go to the bathroom. Guys expect us to do that on a date, anyway. Then come get me. I'll be at the bar scoping things out."

"Okay, Jackie. That sounds like a believable excuse. I'll try that if it's not going well."

"Of course it's a believable excuse. Trust me, girl, you're going to be glad I'm here. Oh look, here he comes."

LANCE PULLED OUT THE CHAIR for Mindy, who smiled as she sat down. "You look even better in person!" he said, as he tried to clasp his hands atop his menu. "Not that you looked bad in your photos."

"Thanks! And no, I know what you mean," Mindy said. "It's a new dress."

"Sorry I couldn't pick you up. My buddy took me shopping for this date," Lance said. "He told me I didn't have any good clothes. He's hanging out at the bar for a bit, to make sure everything's going all right."

"Oh, don't worry about it," Mindy said. "My girlfriend is here too, for the same reason. Are we supposed to tell each other that?"

"Ha, I don't know. To be honest, it's been a long time since I've been on a date."

"Me too!" Mindy said. "It's such a pain filling out profiles and answering questions and all that. Then people only pick matches based on how they look, anyway."

"Hopefully you didn't do that with me," Lance said.

"Not at all—your profile was what caught my eye," Mindy said. "You love *The Notebook* like I do. And some of your pastimes—enjoy cuddling and taking care of cats? That's so cute! Do you have a lot of cats?"

"Oh, well . . . can I be honest? My friend told me to put that in my profile. I've never seen *The Notebook* or read the book. And I actually hate cats. I had one scratch me when I was six or seven, and I never got over it. I always think they're gonna pounce on me."

"So, your profile is just full of lies?" Mindy said, frowning.

"Not totally," Lance said. "Cuddling is okay. And all of the pictures were really me."

"Okay, I guess that's something," Mindy said.

"Do you like Italian food?" Lance said, hoping to change the subject.

"Honestly? Not really," Mindy said. "I mean, I'll have a slice of cheese pizza now and again, but that's about it."

"Wait a minute, your favorite pizza is just plain cheese?" Lance said. "I love pepperoni, sausage, olives, peppers, mushrooms, spinach—heck, even pineapple is good. I don't think I've ever gotten fewer than four toppings on my pizza."

"Yeah, that just doesn't seem appealing to me at all, sorry."

"How about sports?" Lance offered. "Do you play any? Or like to watch?"

"I played tennis growing up," Mindy said. "I've still got a pretty mean lob."

"Oh. That's cool."

"Not a tennis fan, I take it?" Mindy said.

"Not particularly," Lance said. "I find it pretty boring. I've always been a team sports guy."

"Oh, so like football and basketball?" Mindy asked. "Yeah, I guess those are fine. Not for me, though."

"Huh, well, we wouldn't always have to watch sports," Lance said. "Do you like music?"

"That's kind of a silly question," Mindy said, laughing. "Who doesn't like music?"

"Okay, fair enough," Lance said. "What's your favorite genre?"

"Hmm, I think my absolute favorite is hip-hop," Mindy said. "But really, I can get down to just about anything. So long as it's not country. That stuff makes me cringe!"

"Take a guess as to what I listen to almost exclusively," Lance said, looking down.

"Oh no. Is it country?" Mindy said. "It's so terrible!"

"No way. It's great!" Lance said. "Hey, maybe let's eat? That might help loosen things up."

"Okay."

"Let's see," Lance said. "The chef's special—breaded veal and pumpkin gnocchi, with a vegetable medley and a brown sugar and honey glaze drizzled on top. That's for me."

"I'll have a personal cheese pizza, please," Mindy said.

AS THEY FINISHED UP THEIR MEALS, Lance threw his napkin down onto the table. "It's just hard to put yourself out there, you know?" he said. "You're trying to put on a good front for everyone else, and it's like you're almost trying to figure out what *they* want instead of being yourself."

"That's where you're running into issues," Mindy said. "Because then when you show up, you're not anything like who you said you were. And I imagine most women wouldn't like that."

"But that's what my friend told me to do," Lance said.

"Yeah, my friend gave me some pretty terrible advice, too,"

Mindy said. "Let me ask you something. What would be a perfect day for you? If it were just you and you were deciding everything, what would it be?"

"I think I'd love to wake up and do something fun to exercise, like toss a Frisbee around or mini golf, something like that. Then I'd want to have brunch at a place where they bring a mimosa to you for each course. And an afternoon ballgame would be fun, just getting to hang out at the park and watch some good action on the field. Of course, I'd need to get a pretzel at the stadium. It's a tradition! Then before calling it a night, I'd go for a nighttime swim or maybe see a movie at the old drive-in. My parents used to tell me how they'd go to drive-in movies, and I think it's so cool that there's still one here. But I've never actually gone. The idea of it sounds incredible, though."

"See? Now that's a great list of activities for you. Look how happy you got telling me that!" Mindy said. "That's the most excited I've seen you this whole night. Why don't you put that on your profile? Share your ideal date and a woman will know what she can expect."

"Yeah, I did like thinking about that!" Lance said. "But what person would enjoy that?"

"I think a lot of people would enjoy that!" Mindy said. "I know I wouldn't—I can't throw a Frisbee or swim to save my life, and the idea of a ballgame sounds terrible to me. I'd prefer watching a movie at home, too. That way I can get up to use the bathroom or grab a snack. But for the right woman? That sounds like a dream date!"

"So, I just need to be upfront about things?" Lance asked. "That's all it takes?"

"That's not all it takes," Mindy said. "It's not like I'm a dating pro here. But the most fun I've had dating were times we shared experiences that we both liked. It wasn't anything forced, like a fancy dinner. Which, since we're being honest here, is overrated."

"Really? I thought it was super tasty." Mindy smiled at him. "Oh, that's one more thing we don't agree on," Lance said.

"That's totally fine!" Mindy said. "Look, there are people out there for both of us. We'll find them. We just need to be ourselves."

"I like that," Lance said. "Can I give you a piece of advice, too?"

"Sure, what is it?" Mindy said.

"Don't listen to your friend anymore about online dating," Lance said. "She sounds like she's pretty terrible at this stuff."

Mindy looked over at the bar where their friends were sitting, smiling and laughing, touching each other's arm and clinking their glasses. Several empty glasses were lined up in front of them. She turned back to Lance. "It looks like somebody's having fun over there," she said.

"Yeah, look at them go!" Lance said. "Maybe online dating isn't so bad after all."

The Greatest Battle Ever Fought

THE AFTERNOON WAS SUNNY, YET BRISK, AS THE LEAVES IN THE trees had just begun to turn their beautiful shades of red, yellow, and orange. As I often did when engaging in battle, I donned my camouflage jacket. That jacket fit more snugly than anything I've ever owned. It provided incredible warmth, but also allowed me the mobility to scamper across enemy lines—something I did frequently these days. The jacket was a badge of honor, and I wore it proudly.

Today's mission was a pretty simple one. The enemy had something of ours, and we needed to get it back. We'd have to infiltrate their base. It wouldn't be easy, but we could do it. As I waited on our intel, I took a look at some of the other men and women I'd be fighting with. There was Mean Matty Cummings, a guy who could show a sneer on his face that put fear into the hearts of everyone who witnessed it. He could stare down a fighter jet with those steely eyes. I was just glad he was on my side.

Sandy Wilmington was a girl, but I'll be damned if she didn't think like one of the guys. Her potty mouth could put any self-respecting man to shame, while her ability to chase down an intruder was un-paralleled. Credit her parents for putting her through years of soccer practice that had given her powerful legs and a boundless supply of energy. She also had an innate ability to spy on people without getting caught. If I tried to look around a wall, we'd surrender immediately. But Sandy was nearly invisible. And she had the best laugh. While this wasn't really crucial to battle, her laugh was rich, joyful, and infectious, as any good laugh should be. I constantly tried to tell jokes around her, but I only know a handful of wisecracks, and perhaps more importantly, I'm not very funny.

Big Ed was, well, big. That was his calling card. A solid foot taller than the rest of us and at least sixty pounds heavier for good measure. He barely spoke, but when he did, his voice reverberated across the battlefield like a bass in the opera. An encounter with him meant running into a brick wall. He ensured you'd be walking with a limp for a month.

Ashley Patterson had just recently joined forces with us, but she was a welcome addition. Her eagle eyes were so incredible, I'm not entirely sure she hadn't received a transplant from an actual eagle. She could spot anyone out on the field with ease; we called her "Lookout" because of it. That, and because she liked to jump down from her perch—in a tree, on a rock, or anywhere else that was elevated—without any kind of warning at all. If you were nearby, hopefully someone yelled "look out!" or else Ashley would crush you. She was a tiny little ball of a human being, but I don't care how big you are. If she landed on you, it hurt.

Gordon Gaston was one of those guys who was kind of seedy, yet you still liked having him around. He was always able to get intel on anyone we battled, though it was questionable as to how he went about doing so. And to be perfectly honest with you, I don't think we wanted to know his methods. What we could count on was information that was nearly one hundred percent accurate. And in the line of fire, that kind of reliability is crucial. He was the one I was waiting on.

Finally, my best friend, Smelly Riley, rounded out the crew. Smelly earned his nickname because he stunk up a storm. He claimed it was because he only bathed twice a week, which I wholeheartedly believed. We bonded quickly after serving together in the mess hall for a week. Admittedly, I could have befriended anyone amid the awful grunt work of washing dishes and doling out gruel to our peers, but Smelly was an especially good guy. There had been more than a few occasions where we stayed out till all hours, wreaking havoc on the neighborhood and sneaking candy whenever we could. I thought I had a sweet tooth, but Smelly took craving sugar to a new level. He was missing two of his front teeth thanks to cavities. I fortunately still had all of mine intact, though Smelly may have had a better smile than I did, regardless.

It was a formidable group, that's for sure. We hadn't lost a battle yet, and we did not intend to start losing today. Our typical plan was for Smelly and me to attack the perimeter from opposite sides, while Sandy and Gordon ran across the middle of things. Lookout, as she often did, had already mounted a tree to try and scope out weak spots in the defense, and Big Ed stuck around our home base to give us a little extra oomph. I had already lost track of Mean Matty Cummings; I figured he was off somewhere frightening some poor, unlucky sap.

Today, with the air swirling crisply around me, my focus was even more alert than usual. Kneeling behind a large wall with some kind of hieroglyphics written on it, I scanned the field in front of me. About thirty yards away, two men patrolled a blue outpost while a third kept an additional eye on the area. I figured that was our target.

I turned when I felt a tap on my shoulder. It was Gordon. "Got some good news," he said, his shifty eyes darting all over the place. "I've located the enemy base, and it looks like we can capture it pretty easily."

"That's music to my ears," I said. "How many do you think we'll need to secure it?"

His eyes refused to rest in one place. "By my guess, we'll need five of us. Maybe six, just to be safe. They've got a nice little defense around it, but I think we've got the speed and wits to outsmart 'em."

"Okay, grab what we need and get back to our side, then," I said. "No sense in prolonging the attack. Let's get them while they're still resting on their haunches."

BACK AT BASE, LOOKOUT CONFIRMED what both Gordon and I suspected. That blue outpost was most certainly our target. Now our goal was securing it and nabbing the treasure hidden within. If we succeeded, I'd call that a pretty good day, and we could still get home in time for an afternoon snack.

"All right, let's get our strategy mapped out here," I said, drawing a few lines in the sand. "We're going to need everybody for this one, so listen up. Gordon and I will infiltrate from the right-hand side. Big Ed and Lookout? You take the middle. Keep those eyes moving constantly, and alert us if anything seems out of the norm, okay?"

"Aye, aye, Cap'n," Lookout said, giving me an enthusiastic salute. "Nothin' will get past us!"

"Exactly what I wanted to hear," I said. "Now, Mean Matty Cummings, I have no doubts that you can take out an entire army by yourself, but we're not leaving anything to chance here. We're all in. So, Sandy's gonna go with you, all right? Besides, her pretty face will contrast nicely with your ugly one."

Sandy laughed that pitch-perfect laugh of hers. I smiled before turning my gaze to Mean Matty Cummings, who gave me a look that nearly made me pee my pants. "Sorry, bud," I said, shrugging. "But you do have to admit she's better looking than you."

Mean Matty Cummings nodded solemnly. "Too bad pretty don't mean a damn thing on the battlefield." He turned to her. "Just try not to screw things up out there."

"Don't worry, dillweed," she said. "I'll make sure to save a couple of chumps out there so you can feel good about yourself. Maybe I'll even leave a box of apple juice for you."

"Hey now," I said. "This is all very funny, but can we please save the insults until after we've won? Time's a-wasting. Let's move out."

THERE'S A MOMENT JUST BEFORE an attack when everything is quiet. It's serene—eerie, even. Sure, you can hear some sounds, like the wind whistling, the leaves rustling, and your heart beating. But it's mostly quiet. Your adrenaline is about to flow like crazy, but for a brief period, things are calm. I like that moment.

It never lasts for long, though. Usually it's interrupted by an enemy battle cry, as was the case right now. Gordon had stepped through a pile of leaves and gotten his leg caught by one of the enemy guards hiding under the foliage.

Gordon looked down. The guard may have only been about two-thirds of Gordon's size, but he had Gordon's leg in the tightest grasp I'd ever seen. Gordon was planted to the ground as he desperately tried to shake his leg free.

A second defender came to where Gordon was writhing. This second guy was even smaller than the first, but he sure was speedy. He quickly clamped down on Gordon's shoulders. A third guard came to deliver a blow to the stomach. With one final twitch, Gordon looked back at me, his eyes wide. I mouthed "I'm sorry" to him and ran in the other direction.

After what seemed like miles, I was all the way on the left side of the battlefield. I don't know what compelled me to stop running; I guess I figured if someone was chasing me, they would have caught me by now. And there's only so much running you can do before you get tired. "Hey!" a voice yelled behind me. I nearly jumped out of my skin. Nervously, I turned around, ready to bolt at a moment's notice.

Any trepidation I had disappeared when I saw Sandy's face. She laughed when she realized she had scared me. Gosh, that laugh. It was paradise encapsulated in sound. "Hey," I said. "Good seeing you."

"You have no idea," Sandy said. "I am so happy to see you. They . . . they got Matty."

I bit my lip. Mean Matty Cummings, the guy I had once seen fend off eight attackers by himself? The guy who had once made another fella empty his bowels simply by clearing his throat? *He* had gotten caught by the enemy? "You're joking, right?"

"I wish I were joking," Sandy said, "but it's true. Came up right behind us while we were carving up the middle. The big ol' dolt on their side was the one who did it, too. That knucklehead probably has fewer brain cells than a box of crayons. Woulda caught me, too, but Matty pushed me out of his reach. He saved me. I started running so that dweeb couldn't get me, too. Didn't stop until I saw you just now."

"Wow, poor Matty."

Sandy nodded. "While I was running, I heard one of those cretins say that was the third one they captured. Who else have they gotten their hands on?"

"I'm not sure of the third," I said, "but Gordon's gone, too. They surrounded him so fast. I didn't know what to do. I panicked and fled. He must be so disappointed in me."

Sandy grabbed me by the shoulders and looked into my eyes. "Get yourself together, man. We came here to do a job. Yeah, we're gonna lose people along the way. That's the nature of the beast. But don't go feeling sorry for yourself now. Don't matter who's been caught. As long as we're together, we're gonna be all right."

"Look out!" A voice cried from behind us. Sandy and I both jumped back. An enemy was flying right toward us, legs jackknifing through the air. He landed from his makeshift zipline hard on the ground with a thud, groaning in discomfort. A shoe stepped on his chest. I looked up to see who the shoe belonged to—it was Lookout.

"Good timing, Lookout!" I said, smiling. "You always seem to know just when trouble is about to strike."

"Sure do," she said, grinding her heel into the helpless enemy's chest. "It's a talent. But you guys go capture that base. We've lost enough of our team already. No more dawdling. It's now or never. Grab what you need and get out of here."

She was right. If we waited any longer, none of us would make it out. I looked at Sandy and nodded. "Ready?"

"Let's get those scumbags," she said.

We made a beeline for a big tree in the middle of the battlefield. As we arrived, Sandy and I hid, backs to the bark. "What do you see out there?" I asked.

Sandy peered out from behind the trunk. "Not much," she said. "There's one guy sorta hanging around, but he looks like he'd get his undies in a bunch if any sort of ruckus came his way. I think we can take him."

"Then let's lock and load," I said, making a reloading noise with my mouth for extra effect.

Sandy and I darted to the base. We were nearly there when a second guard dropped down, seemingly from out of the sky. Sandy screamed as he descended upon her. As much as I ached to protect her, I knew she'd want me to keep going for the target.

The wind started swirling around me as I outran the final guard to the base. Every step felt like I was fighting an evil force that enveloped me, only I couldn't see it. The harder I pushed, the more challenging it became to move. I gritted my teeth and forced my way to the outpost, grabbing the prize we'd come for. Now I had to get back to our base.

"Stop!" the guard yelled. He turned to his left. "Get him, fellas!"

I glanced around me. Three other guards had stopped what

they were doing and now had their eyes trained only on me. I gulped but knew I had to do this for the rest of the team, especially those who hadn't made it. For Mean Matty Cummings. For Gordon. And for Sandy. Oh, how I wished I could hear Sandy laugh just one more time . . .

Snap out of it, I thought. *Let's get this show on the road!*

I feigned a step to the left to fake out a guard. He lunged toward me, stumbling to the ground as he grasped at nothing but air. From my position, I figured I only had to deke one final guard hanging around and could outrun the others. As I scanned the area, our eyes locked. He glared at me, his eyes squinting under the hot sun. Then I had an idea. I wasn't going to go around this guy. I was going to go right through him.

I charged, my feet moving like a windup toy. I was surprised a cloud of dust didn't kick up behind me with how fast I was moving. Not once did I move my gaze from the enemy guard. Closer and closer I got. Fifty feet away, then forty, then thirty. Now, twenty. I could see the whites of his eyes at this point—and I was showing no signs of slowing down. His mouth twitched, and he clenched and unclenched his fists. I was more out of control than a derailed train. Who would flinch first?

At the last second, he dove out of the way, and I sped right by him, not stopping until I got to our base. Lookout was there to congratulate me on a job well done with a high five. I held the flag high in the air.

In the distance, I heard a voice shout. I smiled at Lookout. "Dang, we are too good at this."

She returned the smile. "We sure are. Same time tomorrow? That's my mom. I gotta go have lunch."

I nodded. Tomorrow seemed so far away, but no matter. We had won this round of Capture the Flag and confirmed our place as masters of the battlefield.

Middle School Dance

IT WAS ANOTHER TYPICAL MIDDLE SCHOOL DANCE. AN UNNOTE-worthy slow song blared over the loudspeakers, some half-hearted decorations adorned the wall, and the gap between the boys on one side of the gym and the girls on the other side was wider than between the waters of the Red Sea when it got parted. None of these people were there at the Red Sea, of course, but a few of them had read about it in class.

"Man, this sucks," Richie Finnegan said. "None of the girls wanna dance."

"I know, man," Martin Hensley replied. "Like, the least they could do is ask us."

Across the gym, the girls were having the same conversation, but with slightly more pity in their voices.

"Just look at them," Marcia Molina said. "Standing there like doofuses. Backs against the wall, mouths open. Just staring at us. What are they staring at?"

"Tell me about it," Rochelle Hambrook said. "The least they could do is come ask us to dance."

At the chaperone table, a decidedly different conversation was happening.

"All I'm saying is you have to consider what the Giants need, you know?" said Mr. Jacobs, the gym teacher. "They need a quarterback. They need a running back. They need receivers. An offensive line. A *defensive* line. A secondary. Linebackers. Their kicking game is great, though."

"Makes sense," replied Mr. Mowdy, nodding his head assertively. He wasn't a football fan or really much of a sports fan at all, so he had no idea Mr. Jacobs had listed virtually every position on the team as a need for his beloved Giants. "You think they can get all those players?"

"That's the thing," Mr. Jacobs said, jabbing a finger into his upturned palm like he was dissecting a treasure map. "If I were in charge, yes, absolutely, we could make it happen. Work the free agent market, trade up in the draft. We'd make moves. But these guys? This GM wouldn't know talent if it came up and bit him on the ass."

"Sounds painful," Mr. Mowdy said, wincing a bit. "If only you were in charge."

"You're telling me, buddy," Mr. Jacobs said, taking a big swig of his punch. "You're telling me."

"I found another booger in the punch bowl," Miss Fontrel said. "That's the fifth one tonight!"

She noticed Mr. Jacobs had just finished his cup of punch, so she tried to soften the blow. "But, um, I'm sure you scooped up your punch before any kids got near it. It's not like children would, you know . . . drink punch at a dance."

Mr. Jacobs was still distraught over the state of the Giants and barely took any notice of what kind of bodily discharges he had potentially swallowed. He stared off glumly into the distance.

"The Giants," Mr. Mowdy said, nodding solemnly. "They'll always get ya."

"Hmm, I suppose they will," Miss Fontrel said. She was a Cowboys fan, but she didn't dare say anything to Mr. Jacobs about it.

He looked like he was close enough to blowing a fuse anyway. "In any case, we need more punch. Do you think you could run and go get some?"

"If it'll get me out of here, sure," Mr. Mowdy said. "What are we looking at here? Two, three bottles?"

Miss Fontrel looked back at the snack table. Billy Busterson was currently lapping up the bowl like a puppy that hadn't drunk anything in days. She turned back to Mr. Mowdy. "Better make it six or seven . . . and get a new bowl, too."

"MAN, WE GOTTA DO SOMETHING about this," Richie said. "I'm sick of just standing here."

"I know, man," Martin replied. "My dad made me put on my good slacks and clean shoes for this. I even put on a tie! And it's all going to waste."

"I was gonna say you're looking fancy," Richie said. "Did you tie that yourself?"

"Of course not," Martin replied. "Got my pops to help out."

"It's a good job," Richie said. "And you know what? He's inspired me. I'm gonna go ask Jaime Parker to dance."

"You got this, man," Martin said. "I'm gonna stay here and hold down the fort. Just in case the ladies come on over."

Across the gym, the girls noticed the boys starting to stir.

"Do you see what's going on over there?" Marcia said. "What do you think they're doing? Think they'll finally ask us to dance?"

"Mmm, I'm not sure," Rochelle replied. "They're up to something, though."

"Look, one of them's walking over," Marcia said, pointing a finger at a figure headed their way. The darkness of the gym, combined with the glittering strobes of the disco balls on the ceiling, made it difficult to see clearly, but the girls distinctly saw someone sauntering over. His shoulders were hunched, and he was walking in an erratic pattern.

"That looks like Richie Finnegan," Rochelle mumbled. "He's kinda cute, I guess."

"Are you kidding me?" Jaime Parker interjected. "Richie Finnegan is *not* cute. He can barely finish a sentence without drooling all over himself. I hope he's asking you to dance, because I won't do it."

Richie walked up to Jaime Parker as she finished her sentence. He could barely lift his eyes up to her.

"Hey . . . hey, Jaime," he said. A small pool of saliva was forming at the corner of his mouth. "Do you . . . do you think you'd be interested in a dance?"

"I'd love to dance," Jaime Parker said, flashing her smile that drove the school's entire male population crazy. "It's just not going to be with you."

"Oh . . . I see," Richie said, his shoulders sagging. "I understand. Thanks for letting me know."

He slowly turned around and headed back to the other side of the gym, his shoes making a dragging noise across the hardwood floor. The other girls began whispering among themselves. Jaime Parker stood tall and firm, a radiant statue of middle-school cruelty.

Marcia nudged her friend. "We should really do something," she whispered. "He looks like he's about to pass out."

"Hey, Richie!" Rochelle called out. "I'd be interested in a dance, if you still want to."

Richie's head whipped around. "Marcia, was that you?" he said, his eyes glistening. "I'd like to dance!"

Marcia glanced at her friend. "Um, no, it was actually Rochelle here. She's a much better dancer than I am, anyway."

"Oh, well I don't know if I want to dance with someone who's really good at dancing," Richie said, scratching his head. "I can barely put one foot in front of the other."

"She can lead you," Marcia said. She was really trying to go to bat for her friend. "Besides, I'm so short. I'd be on my tiptoes the whole time! She's a better dance partner for you."

"If you really think so," Richie said. "But, uh, can I go pee first?"

MR. MOWDY WAS STANDING in line at the checkout counter of the nearby supermarket, holding seven different bottles of punch. He didn't believe in using shopping carts when he was only purchasing a handful of items, because he thought it led to more impulse purchases. He often would buy something like a bag of caramel corn or a jar of pickles even though he didn't really want them. But if he had room in his cart, he had to fill it. It always seemed logical at the time.

Of course, carrying seven bottles of punch is not the easiest thing to do; without a cart, Mr. Mowdy was struggling in line at the checkout. Fortunately, the bottles of punch had those little plastic holders on top of the caps, so he could hold them using just his fingers. He had a bottle tucked underneath each arm and clung to three with his right hand and two with his left. The ones on the right were really getting to him. He kept shifting his weight, hoping that would return the circulation to his fingers. He occasionally sighed heavily to try and expedite the process of the woman two people in front of him, who was taking up all the counter space. She was trying to purchase an exorbitant number of frozen dinners and had a manufacturer's coupon for them that simply wasn't ringing up. Mr. Mowdy nearly yelled out that he'd cover the additional $1.50 for her, but he was focusing all his energy on not dropping the bottles of punch.

After several minutes, the woman was finally on her way. Mr. Mowdy dropped his bottles onto the conveyor belt. They crashed like a drum set falling from a treetop. The man in front of Mr.

Mowdy was only buying a bottle of malt liquor, and after being checked for his ID, he asked if he could also get a pack of smokes.

The woman working the register told him to hold on for a moment while she went to the pharmacy to get his cigarettes. When she left, the man reached a hand around the register and tapped a few buttons. The cash drawer flew open. He didn't want to arouse too much suspicion, so he left some money in the register: a pair of twenty-dollar bills, a few tens, and all the ones.

As he put the wad of cash into his coat pocket, he glared at Mr. Mowdy. "You didn't see nothin', got it?"

Mr. Mowdy had been cleaning his glasses during this entire exchange. His vision wasn't the best, and he was thinking of getting a new pair of glasses. These pinched his nose too much. He placed them back over his eyes. "See what?"

"Good man," the man said, slapping Mr. Mowdy on the shoulder. "Enjoy the rest of your night."

"Thanks," Mr. Mowdy said. "You too!" *Such a nice guy,* he thought.

RICHIE WAS STARING DAGGERS through the mirror in the bathroom. "Okay, Richie, you're going to get out there, and you're going to dance with Rochelle. She's going to think your moves are so cool." He found that psyching himself up was a great strategy that usually worked pretty well. This time, however, he was having trouble boosting his courage. He couldn't understand why. He liked Rochelle. Maybe that was the problem. He didn't *really* like Jaime Parker. She was just the prettiest girl in school. And he didn't *really* like Marcia, he just sat behind her in math class. But Rochelle . . . there was something special about her.

Richie splashed some water on his face. "C'mon, man. It's only a dance. Nobody's asking you to do rocket science or anything crazy like that. You can do it." He turned away from the mirror faster than a dog running to eat dinner. Each step was more confident than the last. He pushed open the door.

"Owww!" a voice cried. Richie peered his head around the door. Mr. Mowdy was rubbing his temple, the bottles of punch scattered all over the floor. "Why'd you come out of the bathroom so fast?"

"Sorry, Mr. Mowdy," Richie said. "I was just really excited to dance, is all."

"Ah, I was young once, too," Mr. Mowdy said, a smile creeping over his face. "You don't have a care in the world. You're able to live freely, no responsibilities, no thoughts of what tomorrow might bring. Everything is encapsulated in that one perfect evening, a dance for the ages. It's really quite magnificent, when you think about it. Sometimes I think back at how far I've come since then. Other times, I feel like I've barely grown at—"

"Um, Mr. Mowdy? Can I go back to the dance now?"

"Oh, I'm sorry. Got a little carried away there," Mr. Mowdy said. "Tell you what—help me carry this punch into the gym, and then you can dance the night away."

Richie nodded. "Let's do it."

He grabbed four punch bottles and bolted toward the gym. Mr. Mowdy had to scramble to catch up. The pair could hear the music getting louder as they approached the gym doors. They burst through them with gusto. "Wow, everyone's dancing!" Richie said. How long had he been in the bathroom? It only seemed like a few minutes. "Look, even Martin's doing it! He said he's never danced before. I gotta get out there!"

Richie and Mr. Mowdy made their way over to the refreshments table. "Okay, Richie," Mr. Mowdy said. "Just help me pour these bottles of punch in the bowl and you're free to go."

"All right, Mr. Mowdy," Richie said. He could barely contain himself. The punch rushed out of the bottle like it was a dam that had just burst open. After the seventh bottle was emptied into the bowl, he turned to Mr. Mowdy. "Okay, can I go now?"

"Now, hold on just a minute," Mr. Mowdy said. "We still have to add some ice and stir it up. Here, grab that bag of ice, and I'll find the ladle."

Richie rolled his eyes. He wasn't sure how he suddenly became the overseer of the punch, but he was now carefully trying to dump ice cubes from an oversized bag into a bowl that was already about to spill over. A couple of cubes of ice trickled out, then a huge chunk propelled itself from the bag. The punch erupted into the air, coating the table and its surroundings—including Richie.

"Mr. Mowdy!" Richie yelled. "There's punch everywhere!"

"Looks like someone had a little bit of a mishap," Mr. Mowdy said, returning with the ladle. He pulled a handkerchief out from his pocket. "Here, let me dab a little. You don't want that to spread."

"Can I go dance now?" Richie said.

"You can, I suppose, but don't you want to see how the punch tastes?" Mr. Mowdy asked. "It's your creation, after all."

Richie angrily grabbed the ladle from Mr. Mowdy. He aggressively stirred the punch, then poured himself a cup. It was perhaps the best cup of punch he'd ever had, but he was too mad to properly enjoy it.

"It tastes great," Richie said through gritted teeth. "Everyone will love it. Now can I please go dance?"

"Of course," Mr. Mowdy said. "Have fun."

Richie stormed off from the table and headed to the dance floor. He surveyed the scene, trying to find a girl who didn't have a dance partner. As he was looking, the music trailed off, and a voice came over the loudspeaker.

"Hey, hey, heyyyyyyyyy," the voice bellowed. "This is your DJ, Dr. Slimebaaaall. Just want to let you know that was our last song of the evening. Thank you all for coming. You've been beautiful. Get home safe and have a greaaaaaaat night!"

Richie looked at the DJ in shock. He had already begun to pack up his equipment. The lights came back on in the gym.

Martin came over to where Richie was standing. "Man, where have you been? Everyone was dancing. It was so much fun!"

Martin had a pink lipstick mark on his cheek. "Who gave you that?" Richie asked, pointing to the remnants of the soft lips that had grazed Martin's face.

"Rochelle Hambrook. Gave me another one on the lips, too!" Martin Hensley said. He playfully threw an elbow into Richie's ribs. "Can you believe it? What a night! I can't believe we didn't dance sooner."

Richie stood gazing out on the floor, dejected. His best friend had kissed the girl he liked. "I missed the whole thing!"

"No, you didn't, man, you got us going!" Martin said. "If it hadn't been for you, none of us would have been brave enough to dance. You're a hero!"

Richie's eyes brightened. "I . . . I am?"

"Yeah, man!" Martin gave him a slap on the back. "Don't get too sad. We'll need you for the dance next month, too. They said it's going to be space-travel themed. That's your favorite!"

"Hey, yeah, it is!" Richie said. "That'll be great. I can't wait for that dance!"

Just then, Jaime Parker came up to the boys. "Hey, dorks," Jaime said. She towered over them, even in flat shoes. Both boys used lifts from their fathers, which still put them about eye level with her shoulders. "I thought this was going to be a really boring night, but I actually had a good time. I guess we have you to thank for setting everything off."

Richie's eyes widened. He really was a hero. "Does that mean you'll save a dance for me next time?"

"Um, no, I will not save a dance for you," Jaime Parker said, a sneer crossing over her face. "I do have standards, after all."

Richie felt his face drop once again. Jaime Parker laughed, like the mere thought of dancing with this short, drooling boy was the hottest comedy act in town. She walked away from Richie and Martin, but after a few steps, she turned back around.

"But I bet every other girl in the school would," she said. "I kept hearing them ask where you were. Maybe you're not as hopeless as I thought."

Richie couldn't help the smile that was now covering his face. "You hear that, Martin? All the girls want to dance with me!"

"I told you, you're a hero!" Martin said. "But go to the bathroom first next time. You were in there for like two hours."

"Oh, I'm not even going to drink anything all day," Richie said. "No water, no soda, no punch, no nothing. I'll be ready to dance all night."

"Sounds great, man. I can't wait," Martin said, throwing an arm around Richie's shoulder. "Let's go get some punch. I need to rehydrate after all that smooching with Rochelle."

Richie froze in his tracks. "How about next time you let me dance with Rochelle?" Richie asked.

"Man, next time you can dance with any girl you want," Martin said. "You heard what Jaime Parker said! You can pick anyone."

Richie smiled. He had never been so in demand. This was the start of a new and improved Richie Finnegan. "I like how that sounds," Richie said. "Now let's get that punch."

As they headed to the table, Mr. Jacobs blocked their path. "Boys, didn't you hear what Mr. Slimeball said? The dance is over. It's time to leave. Us chaperones have lives, too. We can't be keeping an eye on you all night. I have Giants highlights to watch back home."

"Oh, Mr. Jacobs, we were just going to grab some punch," Richie said. "We'll leave right after that."

"Perhaps I didn't make myself clear," Mr. Jacobs said. "You need to leave *now*."

"We can't just take a cup with us?" Richie asked. "It's right over there on the table. We'll be quick."

"Oh, if you'll be quick, I guess that's okay," Mr. Jacobs said. His tone had lightened.

"Thanks, Mr. Jacobs!" Richie and Martin said together. They ran over to the punch table, chugging down several cups of punch. Martin grabbed a couple of large ice cubes from his cup and put them in his mouth, making walrus tusks and snorting. Richie cackled, this low-grade imitation being perhaps the funniest thing he had seen all year.

After several minutes, they each grabbed a final cup and headed toward the door. Mr. Jacobs put an arm out to block them. "By the way, this insubordination means you'll be missing the next dance," he said. "Hope that punch was tasty."

It was. But once again, Richie was in no mood to enjoy it.

The Girl Who Was a Real Flirt at Parties

"CLINT EASTWOOD, RIGHT?"

"That's right!" The man who was dressed as Clint Eastwood eyes lit up. "Nobody has gotten it right yet."

"Well, some of us have an eye for beauty," The Girl Who Was a Real Flirt at Parties said. "When you have a great costume, only the important people will get it."

"Hmm, I never thought of it that way," the man said. "I was just about to take the costume off because I thought it was such a dud."

"Don't do that!" the girl cried. "We need to keep our costumes going."

"Okay, will do!" the man said, nodding aggressively.

"Now come over here. I want to feel what it's like to kiss a real man."

The Girl Who Was a Real Flirt at Parties pulled the man dressed as Clint Eastwood close to her, planting a kiss on his lips. He seemed startled and stumbled back.

"Feelin' lucky over there, punk?" she said, chuckling.

"Uh, sure. Will you excuse me for a moment?" the man asked. "I need to go to the bathroom really quick."

"Gotta take care of Clint Eastwood Jr., huh?" The Girl Who Was a Real Flirt at Parties said. She poked him in the shoulder and winked at him. "You go ahead and do that. I'll be over here on your damn lawn."

She giggled and sat down on the arm of a chair, crossing her legs and arching her back ever so slightly.

The guy raised his eyebrows in a confused look. "Okay? I'll see you around."

"You hurry now!" she called after him. She turned her head slightly to glance across the room. "Oh, hello, Steve from *Blue's Clues!*"

THE GIRL WHO WAS A REAL FLIRT at Parties walked out from one of the bedrooms and headed toward the kitchen. The guy dressed as Steve from *Blue's Clues*—or maybe Carlton from *The Fresh Prince*, it was hard to say, really—soon followed, the faint smear of lipstick on his face. He did a little happy dance and walked in the opposite direction.

In the kitchen, a small group of women were eyeing the counter-top. There were no fewer than five different kinds of chips, all displayed prominently in five brightly colored bowls. The Girl Who Was a Real Flirt at Parties separated herself from the group and went to grab a chip. She opted for the barbecue-flavored chips. Something about them was calling to her. Crooning, almost. Like a love song.

As she placed her hand in the bowl, another hand quickly moved on top of hers. She turned and looked into the eyes of the man whose hand was still touching hers.

"Well, this is quite the handshake," she cooed, giggling uncontrollably. She was up to her fifth vodka and soda of the night already and was feeling giddy. She thought the chips might soak up enough of the alcohol so she could have a sixth drink without too much trouble.

The guy whose hand she was touching smiled.

"Oh, don't mind me, I was only trying to get a chip," he said.

"Well, you got me instead!" The Girl Who Was a Real Flirt at Parties said. She mentally patted herself on the back for how smooth that line sounded.

The guy shook his head, seemingly contemplating if he should walk away from this conversation before he got into too much trouble. "Do you always laugh this much?"

"Only if a funny guy like yourself comes along," the girl said. She had taken her hand out of the bowl and ran her fingers up his arm. When she said "yourself," she gave him a little poke in the chest.

"You know what they say," the guy said. "Sustenance is important, after all."

The Girl Who Was a Real Flirt at Parties stopped and stared at the guy. She couldn't believe what had just come out of his mouth. Finally—someone who understood her!

"Oh my God!" she said. "I was just thinking the same thing. That's why I came over here! It's all about sustenance!"

Her volume rose as she got more excited. "And then I meet a strapping gentleman who's also trying to get a chip. That's fate!"

The guy cocked his head at her, trying to figure out if he should reply or simply pick her up and kiss her passionately. "It is?"

"Yes, yes, yes!" The Girl Who Was a Real Flirt at Parties was almost hysterical now. She was clutching his shirt in her hands. With each word, she gave it a little tug. "This is fate! We were destined to meet and bond over chips."

"Maybe so," the guy replied. "All that because of a chip, huh?"

"All because of a chip!" she said. She took a step back, her hands pressed against her face. She couldn't believe her good fortune.

"Well, that's something," the guy said.

"So, do you like to have a good time?" she said. He was playing hard to get, moving away from where she was standing. She started dancing with him, pressing her body against his.

"I think you're about to fall down," the guy said. "You need to be more sensible."

The Girl Who Was a Real Flirt at Parties stood up straight. She was furious. Who did this guy think he was? "Look! I didn't come to this party to be yelled at. You sound like my dad!"

After that declaration, The Girl Who Was a Real Flirt at Parties stormed off. The rest of her friends watched her leave. One of them tried to call out to her, but she had already gone down the hall in a huff.

"Ooh, that guy makes me so mad," The Girl Who Was a Real Flirt at Parties said to no one in particular. "We were about to eat some chips and make out, and then he has to go and say that. What a downer. Why is he even here? Ugh . . . where did my drink go?"

"YOU'RE A REALLY GOOD KISSER."

The Girl Who Was a Real Flirt at Parties stepped away from the man. She wasn't quite sure what his costume was supposed to be, but he smelled good and had nice lips, so she had taken him into a bedroom to give those lips a test drive.

"Oh, I am, am I?" she said, running her fingers over his arm and flashing a coy smile. "I don't usually do this sort of thing, you know."

"Lucky me, then," the man said. "You're quite skilled at it."

The Girl Who Was a Real Flirt at Parties stepped toward him. She had to stand on her tiptoes to reach his lips, and he craned his neck down to meet her halfway. She cradled his head in her hands, her fingers running through his hair. The soft smacking sound of their lips and tongues was the only noise in the room.

"I'm really glad I came to this party," the man said. "I was going to just stay at home, but my roommates convinced me to come out."

"Stop talking," The Girl Who Was a Real Flirt at Parties said, adding a hiccup for emphasis. "You're cute but you talk too much."

"It's just, I've never met someone like you," the man continued. "You're funny, spontaneous, great to talk with, beautiful . . . and obviously a great kisser." He puckered his lips.

"I'm sorry, what did you say?" The Girl Who Was a Real Flirt at Parties said. She had been distracted looking at a photo on the nightstand. It was a close-up of the party's host with Mark Ruffalo, her favorite actor. "There's a lot going on in this room. It's hard to keep up!"

He smiled. "You're just . . . so amazing. I feel like we have a much deeper connection than making out. It seems like we've known each other our whole lives. There's something about you . . . your aura . . . it's incredibly special. I'm really glad we met, is all."

"Yeah, sure," The Girl Who Was a Real Flirt at Parties said. "You're great, too. So, are we gonna kiss again, or not?"

This Is Art?

"BUT WHAT IS IT SUPPOSED TO BE, EXACTLY?"

"You're so dense, Micah. It's clearly a metaphor for the war. Duh."

My girlfriend Liza gave me a look, like she couldn't believe how stupid I was being. I'd seen that look many times. Usually it was completely warranted, but in this case, I was still dumbfounded.

We were visiting this pop-up art gallery that had recently opened down the block from Liza's place. It featured work from local artists, and ever since it popped up, Liza would tell anyone within earshot how they just *had* to visit this gallery. Somehow, I was the only one she talked into actually going. I guess it was nice to get some fresh air on the walk over to the gallery, and for the most part, the pictures were very pretty.

I liked one where two birds were looking at each other, a worm dangling in between their beaks. It reminded me of an old Western movie, where the hero and villain are about to duel before sunrise. Only this wasn't a battle of life and death; it was merely who would get to eat the worm. The title was a bit predictable—*The Early Birds Get the Worm*—but it still made me chuckle.

I also enjoyed a piece by Ken Dawkins. He was one of my favorite artists; his work frequently appearing in the magazine *Snagg'd*. This watercolor was based off a particularly memorable photograph he had of a kid sliding across the floor to catch a scoop of ice cream that her brother had accidentally knocked off of his ice cream cone. I admired the focus of everyone in the picture. The girl was concentrating on snatching the ice cream from the air. The boy was intently watching his sister. Even the ice cream seemed determined to hit the floor. And Ken had captured that fervor perfectly in his painting.

Those were the pieces I liked. The main attraction, I did not. The brochure said this big, grandstanding image was forty feet tall and one hundred feet wide and took the artist seven years to finish. I just wondered how you got a canvas of that size.

Currently, the main attraction had a mass of people huddled around it. It was hard not to overhear their hushed murmurs, rising and falling with excitement. "Oh, what spectacular use of color!" was peppered with "I can't believe he pulled it off!" with a dash of "Genius, pure genius!" thrown in.

I looked back at the painting. I didn't see it.

The artist, who I could only imagine was a pretentious blowhard, was named Leonard Kensington. I mean, just listen to that name. It reeked of someone who's full of himself. I had never seen any of his work before, but if it was anything like this, I wasn't sure I wanted to.

This particular piece was called *Gesundheit*. Liza was convinced it was a metaphor for war, though nobody around me could agree on its meaning.

"Just look at the corners," one woman said. "Look at what he's expressing there."

"It's such perfect utilization of the space," another man said as he stroked his chin. "I don't think anyone else could do it quite like he does."

I leaned over to Liza. "I'm sorry . . . can you explain again what this is supposed to be?"

She moaned. "Come on, Micah, you seriously can't be that dense. Just step back and take a look at it. And I mean *really* look. Don't think. Don't shuffle your feet. Don't move your eyes. It's only you and the painting. Take it all in. It's beautiful!"

"You can't tell me not to think and then give me a list of things not to do," I said. "That requires thinking!"

Liza rolled her eyes at me. "I can't take you anywhere. I'm going to go stand over here, by the crowd that actually appreciates this art. I'll see you at the car in an hour."

An hour? I had to stare at this painting for an hour? We had already seen everything else in the exhibit. This was the grand finale, and I did not understand it one bit.

I watched Liza storm off to the throng of people pressed up right against the velvet rope that protected the painting, stroking their chins and rubbing their heads in amazement. These were the true fans.

I shook my head. Okay—no more messing around. I was going to figure out what this painting was all about if it killed me. My eyes squinted into a mean glare. My mouth opened slightly, hanging slack as I focused on the huge canvas in front of me.

After a few minutes, a man in a T-shirt and jeans sidled up next to me. He was also here with a girlfriend, who was enamored of the work in front of her. She walked up to join the people at the velvet rope, yelling something about needing to be in the painting's aura.

"What a riot, huh?" the man said to me. "Amazing how crazy everyone's getting for this."

"Yeah, I'm still trying to understand it myself," I said, rubbing my head to try and trigger any sense of comprehension.

"First time at one of these, huh?" the man said, smiling. "Don't worry; they get easier the more you go to them."

"How do you mean?" I asked.

"I still remember my first trip to an art gallery with my girlfriend," he said. "She scolded me because I thought her favorite piece was dumb. And let me tell you, man, it really was dumb."

"What was it?" I asked.

"Literally a guy had hung up two socks on the wall," the man said. "Didn't even use a canvas or paint the socks or even decorate them in any way. Two medium-length white socks with a gray heel. I told her I thought it was dumb that the artist was getting paid for that. She told me I didn't get it."

"That's the same thing happening to me right now!"

"It's okay. You'll figure out how it works," the man said. "Yes, this painting is a tremendous piece of crap. But all you have to do is marvel at it, throw in a gasp or two, and you're set."

"That's really all it takes?"

"I mean, if you want to really dive deep into it, you can try to research a painting or two before you leave," the man said. "Depends how much effort you want to put into it."

"Would that help me understand this piece?"

"Probably, yeah," the man said. "I looked it up when everyone was going wild for it. This asshole sneezed onto a huge canvas. Look at it. You see that little part in the middle there? That's where he blew his nose. His congestion is earning him a bigger commission than you or I will ever see in our lifetimes."

"Oh, so that's why it's called *Gesundheit*," I said, stroking my chin. "You know what? That's pretty clever!"

"See? You're getting it already!" the man said. His girlfriend had walked back over to us.

"Did you make another friend to admire the art with?" she asked.

"Sure did, honey!" the man replied with enthusiasm. His tone had immediately changed. "Neither one of us can believe how incredible this piece is. Really does a great job encapsulating the pain and the anguish the artist was going through."

"That's my man!" the woman said, beaming at me. "Now let's go get that steak dinner you wanted to eat. You've earned it!"

The couple walked off toward the exit, the man winking at me as he passed by.

I ran off to go find Liza. I needed to tell her all the great new things I had discovered about this piece!

Vending Machine Terror

"I'M TELLING YOU, THERE'S NO WAY THEY REALLY EXISTED. THE logistics of it don't make any sense."

"Of course they do! You just have to think outside the box a little bit."

A thin ray of light entered the hallway. Twix and Snickers, who had been debating the legitimacy of the Hanging Gardens of Babylon, turned to face the source.

They saw a heavyset man approach. His name was Gerald, and once a week, he sauntered down the dark hallway to the spot where the vending machine rested. He often had a stain on his shirt, but his light blue button-down today was clean and crisply pressed. The snacks got scared when he came to the machine because he never got the same thing twice in a row. He could order Reese's Peanut Butter Cups one day and select a bag of Fritos the following week. Even the top and bottom rows, which contained various arrays of popcorn and gum and mints, might take a plunge when Gerald was around.

The snacks didn't know what the outside world was like, but they enjoyed the comfort and security the vending machine provided. They got to stick together inside, and there was only one thing they knew for certain: anyone who left the vending machine never came back.

Gerald came up to the display window and put a finger up to his chin, softly repeating the words "Crazy Lover" as the snacks watched in silence. Gerald licked his lips as he pondered the possibilities. The snacks wondered what was going on in his mind. Was he in a candy or a chocolate mood? Or would he go rogue and pick one of the pastry options? Row G was an exquisite buffet of cinnamon rolls, Danishes, and mini muffins.

The contents of the vending machine all looked on timidly while they waited for Gerald to come to his decision. Suddenly, he perked up. It appeared as if he had made his choice. He reached into his pocket for some change. The snacks knew he always carried excessive change in his pocket. Once, they overheard him talking with his coworker Mark, who was the type of guy who would practice his golf swing while having a conversation. Mark had given Gerald the nickname "Maraca" because, with all that change, it sounded like Gerald was shaking a pair of maracas when he walked.

Gerald's face contorted in confusion. He pulled his hand out of his pocket and patted the outside. Then he moved to the other pocket and felt around in there, too. He likely reached into his back pocket as well, though from the point of view of the vending machine, it simply looked like he was scratching his rear end. Desperately, Gerald even peeked into his shirt pocket. It seemed like there was nothing to be found there, either. Somehow, the human maraca didn't have a dime on him. Patting his pockets one final time, Gerald's shoulders hunched in disappointment. He trod off slowly, dragging his feet along the linoleum floor.

Inside the vending machine, the contents began chatting nervously. "Can you believe it? He forgot his money!" said 3 Musketeers, always the optimist. "We're saved!"

"I don't know. Something's fishy here," Twizzlers said, snapping its packaging around with an angry look. "He always has change on him. He *always* does. Hell, that coworker of his called him 'Maraca,' which I've learned about from my readings on the art of Brazilian samba. It's a very loud, jovial instrument. And he was silent today. I should have known as soon as he walked in the door."

A murmur went up among the contents of the vending machine. Surely this couldn't be? Gerald was the most consistent person in the office. He never missed his weekly snack from the vending machine.

"Do you really think he'd wait until next week?" Sour Patch Kids asked. "He's a creature of habit. If he misses his snack today, it could ruin him for the rest of the month."

"Maybe you're right," Twizzlers said somberly. "But I think there's something bigger going on."

Minutes slowly turned into hours. The contents of the vending machine grew restless, nervously anticipating Gerald's return. As evening fell, several people burst through the doorway. The snacks watched intently as the mass of workers grew closer, Gerald leading the front of the line.

Nervous gulps resonated around the vending machine. Whoppers let out a cry of sadness, its box heaving as it wept uncontrollably. Skittles looked morosely over at its cousin, Sour Skittles.

"This is it, everyone!" Hershey's wailed. "We had a good run!"

As Gerald and his colleagues approached, the snacks noticed they were all carrying something. The snacks leaned in closer. "Look at that!" 3 Musketeers yelled. "They've all got cupcakes!"

The snacks heard the workers talking excitedly. "This new afternoon snack policy is amazing!" Gerald said. "We're doing so well as a company that they're actually bringing in freshly baked treats every single day. I'll never have to buy a snack ever again!"

The snacks froze, waiting until the crowd finally passed. As soon as they heard the exit door on the other side of the hallway close, they all began cheering.

"This is amazing! Amazing!" Skittles yelped. "We're all safe."

"You love to see it!" 3 Musketeers said. "I'm so happy I could dance!"

"I guess there is some good out there in the world after all," Twizzlers said.

The snacks hollered and celebrated for hours. They wouldn't have to worry about losing another of their ranks. They finally settled into their slots for the evening, much happier than they had been earlier in the day.

They had just started drifting off to sleep when Twix cleared its throat, breaking the silence. "All I'm saying, Snickers, is there would have been *some* physical evidence of the Hanging Gardens, right? On top of that, nowhere in Nebuchadnezzar's works does he mention anything about a garden."

"The evidence is probably under the Euphrates, and they can't excavate that safely right now. It was a long time ago, you know."

"Ugh, give it a rest!" The other snacks said in unison. "Maybe Gerald will come back for you two."

The Extraordinary Edward

WELL, THIS WAS CERTAINLY GOING TO BE A DREADFUL EVENING.

My girlfriend, Emily, who I thought was kind, loving, caring, and any other sweet adjective you can think of, had decided we were going out to see a show. And not just any show—we were seeing The Extraordinary Edward.

If that name didn't give it away, The Extraordinary Edward is a magician. I hate magic, and I especially hate magicians. They've always got that fake smile plastered on their faces, like they can't believe they're getting paid to play make-believe. And they always have an assistant who looks like she hates her job and is one hundred percent creeped out by the magic maker, but she needs the money for college tuition, so she puts up with his antics. And magicians *always* try to interact with members of the audience in that "let me humiliate you" sort of way. The entire room is in on the hilarious joke, except for the volunteer. No, the volunteer simply gets mocked mercilessly. I mean, how could you not enjoy an evening like that?

Emily, on the other hand, loves magicians. Her dad bought her a card set when she was seven years old, and she thought that would be her career path for years. Once puberty hit, though, she realized she should do something more meaningful with her life. Or at least stop buying new magic sets.

Of course, that didn't mean she stopped performing magic. I have only been with her for about nine months, but she has done about every trick in the book for me. And by "for" me, I mean "on" me. I'd be the lucky guy that got to pick out a card from a pile or would see a dollar bill fly out of his ear. Or I'd get handcuffed to a chair leg, only to instantaneously be freed, so long as I clucked like a chicken.

Emily made all of her tricks seem so grand and elegant, too. She'd announce herself in a big, booming voice. *"Laaaaadies and gentlemen-nnnn . . . are you ready for some maaaaagic?"* she'd say to the crowd. Mind you, the crowd consisted of me and nobody else. Yet, I'd still find myself looking around the room, figuring that at least one of the times she was performing, someone else had sidled up without me realizing. But nope, all of Emily's shows were done for an audience of one. A very uneasy audience of one.

Anyway, I suppose I owed her this. Last weekend we went to a baseball game. Baseball's not my favorite sport, but since it's really the only thing we have in town, we have to make do with it. Besides, there's nothing like a trip to the ol' ballpark. The crack of the bat, the smell of the hot dogs, the loud drunks slurring insults at the players. It's truly a magical experience.

Unfortunately, Emily did not find it very magical at all. On our last visit, one of the loud drunks happened to be right behind us. By the middle of the first inning, he was insulting the opposing team's starting pitcher, a young prospect named Albert Smith, by calling him Fat Albert. In the program I bought, Albert Smith is listed at six-feet-two, 187 pounds. Decidedly not fat, no matter how you define the word. In the bottom of the fourth inning, Mr. Drunk ordered four hot dogs, fully loaded, then proceeded to consume them all before we headed to the top of the fifth. The belches and gas that ensued over the next couple of innings reminded me of being at the bottom of a ball pit as a child. You quickly lose your breath and you do everything you can to get out, but nothing works. It's a sad existence.

In this instance, things got even worse. During the seventh inning stretch, the drunk somehow spilled two separate beers, the contents of which fell entirely onto Emily's head. She tried to laugh the first one off—that was her good-natured spirit shining through. But there's only so much cheap booze you can take to the head before you snap. Since the second spill also resulted in the plastic cup knocking her on the noggin, it's safe to say Emily snapped.

She slammed her arms down in her seat, spun her head around to glare at this man who had made her life a living hell, but found nobody there. The guy had already made a beeline to get more beer, apparently thinking he had finished his. I suppose in a way he had, though I wasn't about to wait around for him to return. I looked over at Emily and was certain I saw smoke coming out of her ears. Forget that the game was tied—we were not going to stay until the end.

"Let's go," I said.

"Great idea," she said, through gritted teeth. "Thanks for a lovely time at the ballpark."

Oh boy. I had heard that tone before. Emily brought it out about twice a month to let me know I had really screwed things up. It had been exactly two and a half weeks since I heard her speak like that, so I was due. We had only been home maybe twenty minutes when she slyly suggested the magic show.

"Have you heard of The Extraordinary Edward?" she said. She was coming out from the shower, her hair still wet. It got a little frizzy when she didn't dry it immediately, which made me very happy. Poofy hair is my favorite.

"No, I haven't," I said. "He certainly doesn't sound like a modest man, though."

"That's really funny," she said. Her facial expression suggested otherwise. "He's coming to town next weekend; he'll be at the Stargazing Theater. I think it would be really fun to go."

"What is he? A comedian? A musician?" I asked.

She shook her head. "Nope, he's a magician." She knew I hated magicians, but she also knew I couldn't say no to this proposal. The look of glee in her eyes made me sick to my stomach.

"Well, if you think it'll be fun," I said. "I'll get us a pair of tickets."

Seventy-five dollars later, there we were, sitting in our seats at the Stargazing Theater. I usually liked seeing music shows there. The capacity was just over four hundred seats, so it was big enough to feel like you were rocking out, but intimate enough to feel like the band was personally speaking to you. But for a magic show? I was just amazed The Extraordinary Edward could even fill up half the room.

The Extraordinary Edward's first trick was a card trick. I couldn't imagine this being much different than Emily's little show, so I leaned back in my chair, not expecting much. And boy, was I right.

"I need a volunteer brave enough to assist me," The Extraordinary Edward called out to the audience. Because card tricks are *so* dangerous. You never know what mysteries you may uncover or what paper cuts you might endure. Only a real fool would volunteer for this.

"I'll do it!" a voice shouted. I knew that voice. It was so familiar, so eager, so . . . oh no. Emily was volunteering to go onstage.

"All right, all right. You look like a wonderful volunteer!" The Extraordinary Edward bellowed as he pointed into the crowd. Fortunately, it was across the theater from where our seats were. I breathed a sigh of relief. Emily was not the one being chosen. I gave her a look that feigned a "tough luck" expression, though on the inside I was dancing.

The "lucky" volunteer ended up being an older woman. She looked like she might tip over at any moment from the excitement. The Extraordinary Edward asked the volunteer's name. "Helen!" she yelled, her voice causing the microphone to howl shrilly with feedback.

The Extraordinary Edward cringed and shook his head. "Helen certainly has the enthusiasm!" he said. "But now let's see if she has the talent to be a successful assistant!" Helen's smile grew even wider.

The Extraordinary Edward thrust a card into her hands and told her to show the camera what it was, so the entire crowd could see it. Nothing fancy. But don't tell Helen that. She moved elegantly, as if she were the queen of England waving during a ceremony. This seemed to be the most important job in the world to her. Clutching the card in her hand like a baby puppy, she let the audience take it in. The card was an eight of clubs.

"Now that everyone's seen the card," The Extraordinary Edward said. "Helen will place it back in the deck. Face down, please." Helen did as she was told, grinning like she was about to open up her first present on Christmas morning. "Now, watch closely."

Holding the deck of cards in his left hand, The Extraordinary Edward wiggled the fingers on his right hand around, moving them up and down. Having seen Emily do this a number of times, and because I have half a brain, I knew this was purely to kill some time during the set. Yet as I glanced around the room, people were sitting on the edge of their seats, mouths agape.

After what seemed like a few minutes, The Extraordinary Edward finally yelled "pow" and slammed his hand into the deck. A barrage of cards fell onto the floor, and an audible gasp escaped the crowd. I couldn't help but think of the poor stagehand that had to clean up all those cards. I've had to pick up the failed remnants of many an Emily trick. I know that those cards stick to the floor like glue.

Helen covered her eyes when the hand came down. After a moment, she came out of her cocoon and looked at the lone card remaining in The Extraordinary Edward's hand. She let out a yelp.

"And now, here's your card!" The Extraordinary Edward said, holding out the eight of clubs to the audience. People got to their feet, roaring their approval. Emily was one of them. I softly clapped, not wanting to give more fuel to this guy. He turned to Helen. "Thank you, darling. You were a wonderful assistant. You may have a seat now."

He placed his hand on her shoulder and left it lingering for just a couple of seconds too long, like a drunk coworker during a holiday party. She still had that huge grin on her face. Good for her, I thought. This probably made her year.

The rest of the show plodded along with the usual array of tricks. Some levitating wagons, a spinning camel, summoning lightning to crash in through a window and strike a match head. Truly pedestrian stuff, really.

After what seemed like an endless barrage of tricks, Emily nudged me in the ribs. "This last trick is the hardest one in the entire world," she whispered to me. "It's the only one I've never been able to fully understand."

"What makes it so special?" I asked. I had seen Emily be confused by several tricks but didn't want to provoke her any further.

"He makes an object disappear!" she said, still looking at the stage. "I've looked everywhere to see how he does it. Magic books, online forums, asking other magicians. There are some bits and elements that people have tried to piece together. Like, they think it's a trap door or a hidden compartment or a mirror or something. But anytime they try to replicate it, they can't do it. Nobody can quite figure it out. I need him to pick me so I can learn how it's done."

The Extraordinary Edward was scanning the crowd for a volunteer. "My assistant this time must be a very brave soul," he said. "You must have nerves of steel and the ability to stay cool under pressure. Because, ladies and gentlemen, for my final trick, I am going to make one of you disappear into thin air."

Looking over at Emily, I thought her shoulder was going to shoot right out of the socket. Her arm couldn't possibly have been any higher in the air. She had a look of desperation to be chosen in her eyes, as if she were one of the last two people left in gym class while the more popular kids were picking teams. There's no shame in being the second-to-last selection, but people remember who was picked last. If Emily didn't get chosen here, it would be even worse than being picked last—and it would make for one uncomfortable ride home. I concentrated my thoughts, trying to give Emily some positive energy.

The Extraordinary Edward gazed across the room. He seemed to be studying a few possibilities, mulling over who would be the perfect volunteer. He was a flamboyant showman and milked this selection process for all it was worth, asking sections to cheer loudly if they felt someone in their row should be chosen, and holding a hand up to his ear during the roaring response.

When he was finally finished traipsing around the stage, encouraging the crowd to hoot and holler until they were hoarse, The Extraordinary Edward looked at us. First at me, then at Emily.

"Ladies and gentlemen, I have made my decision! You there," he pointed. "You come up here."

Emily's jaw dropped. She looked over at me. I looked back at her, then up at The Extraordinary Edward. He was not pointing at her. He was pointing at me. That long, disgusting finger, which was probably covered in dirt after performing all this magic, was staring me in the face.

"Nah, I'm all right where I am," I said. "She'd love to be your volunteer, though." I gestured to Emily, who had turned a deep shade of red. Apparently, being singled out was only acceptable if The Extraordinary Edward was the one doing it.

"I didn't ask her," The Extraordinary Edward said, a dead smile frozen on his face. "I have chosen you. You'll make the perfect assistant, and unfortunately, I'm not going to take no for an answer."

This seemed incredibly out of line to say to a paying audience member. I was still planted firmly in my seat. But Emily grabbed my wrist.

"Go," she said. "Do it for me. Be the best assistant you can be." With those reassuring words, I slowly got to my feet.

You know when someone gets called to "come on down" on *The Price Is Right?* And they barrel down the aisle like they're the giant rolling boulder and Contestants' Row is Indiana Jones? It's a wonderful spectacle to behold. My gracing the stage of the Stargazing Theater was the exact opposite of that. I trudged, my feet making unpleasant scraping noises as they slid across the floor. I felt the eyes of every audience member on me and suddenly wished I had worn a nicer shirt. Or at least that I hadn't missed that one spot on my chin while I was shaving that morning.

Emily was cheering louder than anyone in the entire building. I thought she was going to get thrown out for causing such a stir. As I finally climbed the top step and walked across the stage, I made eye contact with her. She was definitely happy for me, but it seemed like just the tiniest bit of her wished she were on the stage instead. I shrugged and mouthed *I tried.*

The Extraordinary Edward held out his hand. I didn't know if he was gesturing for me to stand at a certain spot onstage or if I should shake his hand. I went for the handshake, grabbing his hand tightly and even throwing in a gentle elbow touch with my other hand. It turns out I'm not very good at reading people's minds. He was caught off guard. "Oh, I was just gesturing for you to stand over there," he said quietly to me.

I took my place where The Extraordinary Edward gestured. He loudly proclaimed to the audience, "This man was brave enough! Brave enough to come onstage as a volunteer who knows he's going to disappear!"

I couldn't help but think that his use of the term "volunteer" was loose, at best. I also didn't believe I'd actually disappear; Emily had just told me about this trick. I smirked. The Extraordinary Edward took notice. "Someone seems skeptical!" He was certainly a perceptive fellow, if nothing else. "Let's see if we can't change your mind."

I heard a loud noise behind me. Turning around, I saw The Extraordinary Edward's assistant—the actual assistant, not wonderfully naïve Helen—pushing a large box on wheels. She came up to me while Edward continued blabbering to the crowd.

"Just step right in here," she said, unlatching the front. "Don't worry, you won't feel a thing."

The inside of the box was, by my guess, seven feet tall and four feet wide, and maybe about two feet deep. That wouldn't give me very much wiggle room at all. "It's a little bit of a tight squeeze, isn't it?" I said, without stepping inside.

"You're not going to be in there for very long," she said, nodding her head at the box. There seemed to be an air of impatience in her tone. "So, you know, you can get in anytime."

I sighed and told myself I was doing this for Emily. I turned and smiled at her as I squeezed into the box. She was starstruck, beaming at The Extraordinary Edward. He finished his grand speech about the space-time continuum and moved next to the box.

"Try not to scream," he said, and cackled. "It makes the disappearing that much more painful."

This was starting to get ridiculous. I was quite looking forward to getting out of the box. The Extraordinary Edward shut the door. Instantly, I was surrounded by darkness. I kept waiting for my eyes to adjust. They didn't. I could still hear The Extraordinary Edward talking, but I couldn't make out what he was saying. I'm sure he was giving another grandiose speech. The man would have no trouble with a public speaking career. He could make any mundane topic sound exciting with his wild gestures and emphatic syllables.

Suddenly, my shoulder started swelling up. *No big deal*, I thought.

After all, I had been playing flag football pretty regularly, and this last week I took a nasty fall making a sideline catch, landing right on my shoulder. The adrenaline of the game kept me going, but ever since, it would periodically throb. That's all that was happening, I bet.

The pain was getting deeper, though. I reached with my hand to try and massage the shoulder, but I couldn't move. The box was too tight. While I tried to distract my mind from my shoulder pain, I noticed my left foot had become incredibly itchy. I slid my shoe around as best I could, but this was an itch that needed a fingernail, preferably all ten fingernails, to scratch. The irritation was driving me nuts.

As I continued wiggling my toes around, my eyes started watering. They were burning, too. It was like someone was chopping onions in front of my nose. This was horrible, I thought. I debated banging on the box. Something had to be going wrong.

I raised my fist to knock on the door and realized I couldn't hear The Extraordinary Edward anymore. In fact, I couldn't hear anything. Had the trick already happened? It hadn't been more than a few seconds. Maybe that was all the time it took to make someone disappear. It certainly wasn't an enjoyable process. I tapped my fingers lightly on the box. To my surprise, the door flew right off.

Gingerly, I placed my itchy left foot outside. As soon as it touched the ground, the itching subsided. As I stepped out of the box, all of my ailments vanished.

My feet seemed to be mired in some sort of sand, though this was unlike any other sand I'd ever seen. It wasn't sticking to anything and was almost a pure yellow color. I reached down and picked up a little bit in my hand. It sure felt like sand. Maybe it was normal sand that someone had taken the time to dye. People have hobbies. Perhaps whoever did this just had a really odd hobby.

There didn't seem to be much of anything around. I noticed a few lights way off on the horizon, but they might have only been stars.

Outside of those small, dim lights, there wasn't a single thing around, as far as I could tell.

As I let the sand fall from my fingers, I noticed a constant humming in the distance, like a dryer. It reminded me that I needed to do laundry when I got home.

My eyes locked onto something in the sand. Maybe five inches long, a shiny yellow color, almost like a jar of mustard. It stood out even in the yellow sand. I peered closer. It was curved a little bit, and it had something sticking out from the end of it. That something, whatever it was, had twined itself around the middle. I could barely make the object out.

"Are you there?" a voice called. Startled, I snapped my head up. Craning my neck, I looked in every direction. There wasn't a person in sight. But I didn't imagine that. I *knew* I'd heard something.

"Can you hear me?" the voice said again. This time I thought I'd try to answer back.

"Who said that?" I yelled up at the sky. "Where am I?"

"Listen very carefully," the voice said. "This is The Extraordinary Edward. First of all, I want to tell you that you did a terrific job as my volunteer. I'm very proud of the effort you put forth, and in case you couldn't hear, the crowd went wild. They loved it!"

That's exactly what I was concerned about. I had no idea where I was, but at least the magic trick was a crowd pleaser. Perfect.

"So, the show's over?" I asked. "I can go home now, right?"

There was a long pause. I heard The Extraordinary Edward take a deep breath before he began speaking. "Yes and no," he said.

"Um . . . what . . . what do you mean?"

"You see," The Extraordinary Edward said, "this was my biggest show yet. Can you believe two hundred and seven people came tonight?"

"I don't care about sales numbers, man," I said, with a hint of exasperation. "Where am I and how can I get back to the theater?"

"I'm going to explain everything. Just please listen," The Extraordinary Edward said. "Like I was saying, this is the biggest show I've ever done. And because of that, I wanted to close with a trick that would really wow the audience. It would completely blow their minds. It would be unlike anything they've ever seen before. That's why I chose to make someone disappear. And from my first trick, I knew it would be you. You had been rolling your eyes the entire night. You didn't believe. You were a skeptic. Your attitude made you the perfect subject for my final trick. I knew if I could convince you of the power of magic, I'd have done my job.

"But this trick is quite difficult to pull off. It tested my greatest strengths as a magician. I've performed it before on inanimate objects and on mice and birds, but never on a human. You were my first. You should be very proud of that. You were a part of history!"

"Congratulations to me," I said. It was kind of cool to be a part of history. "Wait, why did you say 'were'?"

Another long pause. "I'm sorry, I don't know how to put this, but. . . . How about we try it this way? There was a complication with the trick. You see, I hadn't accounted for your body mass. Like I said, I've only done it with small objects, mice, and birds. With that calculation altered . . ."

I did not like the sound of this. "You're going to finish that sentence, right?"

"With that calculation altered and based on our conversation right now, it seems like you're currently in between two universes, stuck in some kind of suspended animation."

"What?" I said. "But this is just a snag, right? You'll get me back to the right universe soon."

This pause was the longest. "I'm afraid I'm not sure how to do that."

I rubbed my hands over my eyes and shook my head. Maybe if I shook hard enough, I could get back to reality. This had to be a joke. "I'm sorry, *what* did you say?"

"This happened with the mice and birds, too," The Extraordinary Edward said sheepishly. "I could make them disappear, but I never did find out how to get them back."

"So, you're telling me that you've never actually performed this trick successfully, and you still tested it on a human being!" I was screaming at the sky now, my voice cracking.

"Oh no, the tricks were quite successful. The animals always disappeared. And you did, too. In fact, I'd say my success rate for this trick is one hundred percent!" The Extraordinary Edward said. "It's just the unfortunate matter of making you re-appear. That's where I'm a little less proficient."

I sunk to my knees in the sand, my hands clutching the sides of my head. I thought about Emily. How I wished I could talk with her. I wondered if she was worried about me. But then my thoughts turned to her in the crowd. How she had probably cheered when the box opened, and I wasn't in it. She probably stood up, too, joining the audience in a standing ovation. None of them knew where I had gone. Nobody likely even gave it a second thought. I was completely alone.

"Can you tell me about the place you're in now?" The Extraordinary Edward asked. "What do you see?"

From my knees, my eyes connected with the yellow object from earlier. I brushed aside some sand and picked it up. A knot formed in my throat. There, in the palm of my hand, was a bird's beak, with a mouse's tail emerging from the opening.

Special Request

IT'S ACTUALLY RINGING.

I had been calling into the Sammy Slimeball Show for more than three years. Not every day, of course. That would be pathetic. But on Saturday nights, Sammy Slimeball and company would do an hour of nothing but requests. Callers could pick out any song. Sammy Slimeball would play it for them, let them give a dedication, and even introduce the song themselves, if they really wanted.

Whenever I had called in previously—which, again, hadn't been *that* often, just every Saturday for a few years—I was greeted with a busy signal. Sometimes I'd hang up and give it another go. After all, I understood the station was inundated with callers. Occasionally, I simply hung up and listened to people make their choices. Usually I dug what they selected, but there were instances when I bet Sammy Slimeball regretted letting certain people on air with their decisions.

I was going to be different, though. I had my song picked out for weeks and knew exactly what I was going to say to Sammy Slimeball. It was so great, in fact, I wouldn't be surprised if he told me to stay on the line so he could offer me a job after the show. It was going to be—

"Sammy Slimeball Show, can you please hold for a minute?"

I began responding with an "of course," but hold music had already started playing on the other end. *Oh, they're busy,* I thought. Besides, this was further than I had ever gotten before. I could barely contain my excitement and felt my heart pounding away in my chest.

This call could change everything. All those times I'd dialed in, a busy signal ringing in my ears. I had been able to time out the length of the beeps in my head, a skill I picked up over the years. My co-workers thought I was being silly, calling in all the time, avoiding going out on the weekends. Then again, it's not like they ever invited me along on their happy hours, so what else was I going to do? Now, I was going to get the last laugh. My hard work and persistence were about to pay off big time.

About twelve minutes later, that same voice came back on the line. "Thanks for calling into the Sammy Slimeball request hour. What do you want to hear?"

"Hi, Sammy!" I said enthusiastically. "Thanks so much for taking my call. I'd like to hear—"

"Look, kid, I'm not Sammy." It sounded like he was rolling his eyes as he said that. "I'm one of five producers on the team here. You don't think Sammy does this all by himself, do you?"

"Of course not!" I said, an indignant tone rising in my voice. "He's got Pickle Pete, Jenna Jam, Stooby in the Street . . ."

"Yeah, and *they've* got all of us working behind the scenes to make sure they don't screw things up," the voice on the other end of the phone said. "And even with all of our help, they usually still manage to blow it. Anyway . . . what song do you want to hear?"

"I would love to hear 'Crazy Lover' by Edwin . . . Edwin . . . wow, this is a little embarrassing, but I seem to have forgotten his last name!" I said, throwing in a little chuckle to show how playful I could be on air. "I really do love that song—maybe just a bit of stage fright, here."

"Yes, sir, I know what song you're talking about," the producer said. "But you'll have to pick another one. Someone else has already requested it. Ever since that guy released his new song, somebody calls in to ask for 'Crazy Lover.' I personally can't stand the tune, but hey, what do I know? I just push some buttons."

"Oh man, that's a real disappointment," I said. "Let me think for a minute—I don't have a backup in mind."

"Try and think quickly," the producer said. "We have a lot of people calling in."

"Of course," I said. "Hmm . . . oh! I know! How about one of MC Cemetery's early hits? I loved that duet he did with Edwin, and I checked out his whole collection of songs. They're really good!"

"Yeah, they're not bad," the producer said. "Unfortunately, ever since he retired from making music, he's actually asked radio stations to stop playing his songs. Too many bad memories, he said. We're a classy venture here, so we're going to honor his request."

"Oh, I didn't know that," I said.

"He's been trying to keep it out of the news. Really doesn't want people knowing about him anymore. His funeral business has taken off, but he still keeps a low profile. Great guy, truly. Shame about his music career. Anyway . . . you'll have to pick another song."

I was really getting flustered now. My musical knowledge was escaping me. I could sing you more than ten thousand songs, but for whatever reason not a single one was coming into my head. I quickly got onto my computer and started a search for "good songs to request on radio."

"Sir, are you searching for a song?" the producer asked. "I can hear you frantically typing over there."

"Uh . . . no, of course not," I said. "Don't be silly!" I waved my hand in the air, like people do when they're shooting down crazy ideas. The momentum of my swat carried my hand into the computer screen, and a sharp shooting pain coursed through my fingers.

"So . . . do you have a song?"

"Uh, yes. How about 'Smart and Smarmy' by The Ottersmocks?" I couldn't believe what I had just said. The Ottersmocks are campy. Novel. Juvenile. Trite. Their sole mission is writing cheesy pop lyrics that appeal to teenagers. Most of the time, they even fail at that.

"You've gotta be kidding," the producer said. "Look, I understand you're feeling some pressure here, but I'm gonna have to take a stand. This station has never—not once—played a song by The Ottersmocks. We pride ourselves on putting good, quality music on the airwaves. Now, I know this is the all-request hour, and I really do want you to get a nice song played, but I think we'll both agree—anything by The Ottersmocks is not that song."

"Yes . . . yes, I understand. Sorry for suggesting it."

"Hey, it happens to the best of us," the producer said. "How about this? I'll choose a song for you, and when you get on the air, you can have Sammy Slimeball 'pick' one for you. He loves doing that. Always good banter between him and the guest. How does that sound?"

"That sounds great!" I said. "I'd love to chat with Sammy. What song are you going to pick?"

"I'd hope you want to talk with him, if you're calling into his show," the producer said. "And I obviously can't tell you the song. It's supposed to be a surprise."

"Ah, of course," I said. "Looking forward to it!"

I anxiously glued the phone to my ear the rest of the show. I did get to hear "Crazy Lover," which was great, though I thought the guy calling in was quite the dud. He didn't even say "cah-RAAAAA-zy lover" like you're supposed to. Talk about dropping the ball!

Other songs played without much fanfare. It seemed like a particularly low-key Saturday night. The requests were mostly oldies, which isn't a bad thing, though a lot of them I had never heard before. That's always a bit of a bummer—how else can I sing along?

"Alriiiight, you crazy crew of listeners," Sammy Slimeball's voice boomed over the airwaves. "This is our last caller of the all-request hour."

I sat up in my seat and straightened my shoulders. I cleared my throat and shook my head about, working out the kinks in my neck. I took a deep breath to make sure my diaphragm was nice and relaxed for my big radio debut.

"Yes indeedy, our final caller of the night," Sammy Slimeball bellowed. "Let's go to Sally in Michigan! Sally, how are you doing?"

A voice responded to Sammy Slimeball that she was doing well, though she was a bit cold. I slumped back down in my seat, my heart sinking. How could they have forgotten about me?

"Hello . . . hello?" a voice on the other end of the phone said. "Are you still there?"

"Yes, I am! Sammy!" I yelled. "Oh, I knew you'd take my call!"

"Um . . . no, this is the producer," the voice said. "Just wanted to apologize that we couldn't get you on tonight. We always take a few extra callers in case someone gets disconnected or has stage fright or a really short conversation. Something like that. Better to be safe than sorry, right?"

"Oh . . . yeah, I suppose that makes sense," I said, though I didn't think it made any sense at all. "How many other callers didn't make the cut?"

"You know, it's actually kind of funny," the producer said. "You were the only one who didn't make it on air tonight. Normally we have about four or five who don't, but all these callers sped through their conversations pretty quickly."

"But . . . but couldn't I talk to Sammy now? Since there's only me left?"

"Sorry, pal," the producer said. "No can do. We run a pretty tight ship here. Once the all-request hour is done, we gotta move on."

"Oh . . . okay. I guess I understand." Again, I did not. "Wait, can I ask you one other thing?"

"Sure, go for it."

"What song did Sally in Michigan choose?"

"Oh man, it was a real terrible way to end the show," he said, taking a deep breath. "I feel awful that it happened. She picked The Ottersmocks."

"But . . . but I thought we weren't allowed to request that!"

"Yeah, one of the other producers took her call. And that one apparently likes The Ottersmocks, so she let it slide. Talk about a real downer. I'm still sad about it."

"Oh, okay, I guess," I said. "Thanks for giving me the chance to almost speak with Sammy Slimeball."

"Anytime," the producer said. "Thanks for listening to the Sammy Slimeball Show's all-request hour. Feel free to call in again next week."

The Big Shot

DOUG MADISON HAD GOTTEN QUITE COMFORTABLE IN HIS SEAT at the end of the bench. As the fourteenth man on the Lawson Leopards, currently the fifth-best high school basketball team in the district's division (out of a robust seven teams), he had never made it into a game. He didn't mind, though. Just being on the team was cool enough.

At practice, his teammates called him Dig Doug because of his penchant for chasing after opposing players like they were monsters in the arcade game of a similar name. He also once spent the entire practice excitedly talking about a time capsule he had buried in the park earlier that day.

Doug wasn't enjoying this game very much, though. The Leopards were facing off against the Town Park Toros, who had only lost two games all season. Tonight would not be the third. The Toros had a fifty-two-point lead by halftime, and as the third quarter came to a close, the score was 84–21.

Doug was the first one on his feet to greet his teammates. The horn had barely sounded to signal the end of the quarter, and he was already at half-court, slapping hands and giving encouraging chatter. He couldn't keep track of how many times he yelled a "Let's go!"

or "You can do it!" during the season. He knew what part to play on the team—that of the lovable goof that could lift spirits up, even in the darkest of times.

"Thanks, Dig Doug," Rufus Ledletter said, lightly bumping Doug's outstretched fist. Rufus was the star senior on the team but, like the rest of the Leopards, was having a rough night. He had missed his first eleven shots and was currently sitting at only four points. He hadn't scored fewer than ten in any game this season.

Doug hurried over to Coach Morris, who was dejectedly scribbling a play on his miniature dry-erase board. Halfway through, the ink ran out in his marker. It was a fitting symbol of how terribly this game was going. Coach Morris sighed heavily. He looked at his players. "Just don't screw up too badly, okay?"

The five players taking the court headed back out there, and Doug clapped wildly. After a moment, he realized he was still standing on the court and everyone else had already taken their seats on the bench. He scuttled back to his spot at the end.

With about two minutes remaining in the game, the Leopards had actually closed the gap. It was now 95–38, a mere fifty-seven-point deficit. Rufus had just scored to reach ten points, continuing his streak of double-digit performances.

"Madison," Coach Morris called out. "Get in there for Ledletter."

Doug heard the words, but they didn't register. He took a sip of water and kept looking out toward the court.

"Madison!" Coach Morris bellowed. "You're going in! For Ledletter."

Doug froze. This was uncharted territory. Sure, he played during practice, but in an actual game? He looked deep into Coach Morris's eyes, hoping for some sort of empathy.

"Well?" Coach Morris said, smacking his chewing gum across his lips. "Get going!"

Doug got up and trudged over to the scorer's table. Maybe he wouldn't even make it in the game. After all, the clock was ticking down, and if there wasn't a foul, a ball out-of-bounds, or a timeout, he'd just stay at the scorer's table and wouldn't have to go in the game. That wouldn't be so bad at all.

THWEEEEEEET!

The whistle blew. So much for that. The Leopards had committed a foul, so Doug was coming in. He got up from his crouching position at the table and started a slow walk onto the floor, his knees buckling with each step. He pointed at Rufus. "R-Rufus," he stammered, his voice cracking, "I'm coming in for you."

Rufus came over to him and gave him a pat on the chest. "Hey man, breathe. It's just basketball."

Doug nodded. It was just basketball, after all. So why did his legs feel like jelly?

He found his man. Number 22. Doug looked up at him; this guy was a few inches taller and several pounds heavier. But Doug was determined. Number 22 wasn't going to score. Doug placed a hand on his opponent's hip. Number 22 slapped it away. Doug put his hand back on the guy's hip. Number 22 cut hard to get open, but Doug was right there. He had never been so focused in his entire life.

Number 22 caught the ball. Doug was so close to him, he got a mouthful of jersey. It tasted salty. Number 22 dribbled four times, then passed the ball to a teammate. Doug relaxed for a second.

But Number 22 got the ball right back and Doug tensed up again. He was so high on the balls of his feet, it was almost as if he were floating. Number 22 dribbled to his right, and Doug slid along with him. He reached to knock the ball away and—

Wham!

Doug hit a brick wall. Or, at least, that's what it felt like. He had actually hit the Toros' center, a big hulking lug of a man.

There is no way that guy is under 30 years old, Doug thought, lying dazed on the gymnasium floor. He blinked his eyes several times, trying to shake off the cobwebs. As he rolled his head back and forth, he started hearing something. It was faint at first, but soon it got louder.

"Doug! Doug! Doug! Doug!"

The crowd . . . They were actually chanting *his* name. He couldn't believe it. Not only was he making his first career appearance in a game, he now had an entire group of people cheering for him. He leapt to his feet, raising a fist in the air and pumping it over his head. The crowd roared its approval.

Thirty-four seconds left on the clock. The Leopards were getting the ball back, and Doug knew what he had to do: make the game-winning shot.

Well, it wouldn't really be the game winner. But it sure would feel good to see the ball go through the hoop after leaving his hands. He took the inbounds pass and started dribbling up the court. Across from him, Number 22 was digging in, playing defense without giving up an inch.

Doug's teammate Mike Stoudamire was standing with his hands up. Mike was Doug's best friend on the team, mostly by proximity. Mike sat one spot ahead of Doug on the bench and rarely made it into the games either. But he had scored before. This was Doug's moment.

"I got this," he said, waving Mike off.

"Okay, man," Mike said. "Whatever you say."

He ran over, setting a screen on Number 22. That caused just enough of a ruckus to get Doug open on the wing. Number 22 was clawing his way around the screen. Doug saw another defender flailing toward him. This was his chance.

He squared up to the basket. The crowd was on its feet, stomping on the stands, clapping their hands, whooping and hollering. Doug sensed they could tell they were about to witness something remarkable.

Doug lifted his arms. The ball felt weightless in his hands. He took one last glance at the oncoming defender, then rose up and snapped his wrist, releasing the ball at the apex of his jump. It was perfection. One magic moment. The crowd silenced itself instantly, the cheering turning into an excited hush.

As the ball came off his fingers, Doug felt everything moving in slow motion. He became acutely aware of what was happening around him. Number 22 was standing to his right, his hand outstretched in a valiant yet failed effort to block the shot. The other defender lunging toward Doug stopped and turned, his eyes fixated on the ball.

Mike, who had rolled toward the top of the key after setting the screen, was staring at the ball as well, his mouth slightly open. One of Doug's other teammates, Louis Finnegan, had been battling with a defender down low before the shot had gone up. But now, with the orange sphere hurtling toward the rim, the two of them momentarily paused, their arms intertwined. Neither one of them noticed their locked appendages.

Doug glanced over to the bench. Rufus and the rest of the starters had risen to their feet, their eyes tracking the path of the ball. Even Coach Morris had stopped yelling for a moment, his open mouth revealing a wad of gum that had been chewed far too aggressively.

The ball was in the air for what seemed like an eternity. Doug looked toward the stands. He saw his buddy Chris, who had come to the game with his girlfriend Christine. Doug always teased Chris about dating a girl with the same name. Chris would get mad and tell Doug, "At least I have a girlfriend." Doug didn't have a counter for that.

Near Chris was Zack, who was kind of a jerk. He had bullied Doug, among several other nameless victims, throughout junior high and high school. He smelled of stale beef jerky and loved to creep up behind Doug while he was grabbing his books, slamming the locker door in his face. Maybe now Doug could get some respect from Zack.

And there, two rows behind Zack, was Vanessa. Oh, Vanessa. Doug sat behind her in English class, and it was the best forty-two minutes of his day. They were reading *The Grapes of Wrath*, and their teacher would call on students to read passages in class. When Vanessa read about Rosasharn and the rest of the Joads dreaming of a better life in California, Doug's heart simply melted. Sometimes Doug would forget his pencil on purpose so he could ask to borrow one from Vanessa. She'd smile as she took an extra one out of her pencil case. "Okay, but don't lose it," she always playfully warned. Doug wouldn't dare lose it. He would cherish that pencil for the entire class.

But right now, none of that mattered. Doug was going to score his first points as a varsity athlete. This was going to be the start of something big. This could change his whole life.

The ball was nearing the hoop now. Every single player had stopped and was following its arc along with Doug. He had finally come down from his jump, his feet softly landing. He got new shoes before the game and loved how comfortable they felt. He couldn't help but smile as the ball launched toward the backboard.

And went right over it.

The horn sounded as the ball harmlessly bounced out of bounds. An audible groan rose from the crowd. Doug had missed. Badly. An airball. He couldn't have hit something, *anything?*

Doug scanned the gym again. His teammates on the bench winced, shaking their heads. Coach Morris had resumed chewing his gum again, seemingly grateful to get this game over with. He distinctly heard Zack's laugh in the crowd; he turned to find the bully's long finger pointing at him. Chris and Christine gave a sympathetic wave, but Doug didn't see Vanessa anywhere. Doug breathed a sigh of relief. Maybe she'd forget all about that miss by the time Monday's English class rolled around.

The gym slowly emptied out. Various teammates and opponents came up to Doug, tapping him on the shoulder and telling him he played a good game. He heard them saying words but couldn't quite process them, maintaining a thousand-yard stare all the while.

After a while, Doug was the last one left in the gym. He decided it was finally time to go home; he wanted nothing more than to crawl into bed. As Doug walked toward the door, the school janitor entered from the other side of the gym. "What are you still doing here?" the janitor yelled across the floor.

"Oh, just reflecting on the game, I guess," Doug said.

"Yeah, that was a tough one to watch!" the janitor said. "Those Toros sure can play some ball."

"They sure can," Doug said. "Anyway, sorry to startle you. Have a good night."

"Wait a minute, is this yours?" The janitor started bouncing a ball from the corner of the gym. Doug's air ball had rolled so far away from the basket that no one had thought to pick it up.

"That's from the game," Doug said. "If you want, I can drop it off in the locker room on my way out."

"That'd be great!" the janitor said. "I'm just doing my nightly sweeping, and then I'm out of here, too. Time to get the weekend started."

The janitor took a few more dribbles out onto the court and flung it toward Doug, standing on the opposite baseline. The ball soared through the air and whipped through the net. The sound of the swish reverberated through the gym.

"Ha! Would you look at that?" the janitor said. "I was just trying to get it over to you, and it went through the hoop. How far away do you think that was?"

"The length of this court is eighty-four feet," Doug said, his face locked on the hoop where the janitor had just made a full-court heave. "You just sunk a shot from almost a hundred feet away."

"Oh, that's funny," the janitor said. "Guess I should have been out on the floor tonight!"

He chuckled as he retrieved his broom and started whistling a tune as he swept the gym floor. The ball had finally come to a stop a few feet from Doug. He sighed and left the gym. The janitor could pick up the ball himself.

Please Remain Seated

———

"REMIND ME AGAIN HOW I LET YOU TALK ME INTO THIS."

"Because it's going to be *fun*, silly!"

I had a hard time believing that, yet there I was with my friend Laura in line for the Shredder, otherwise known as the speediest, most complex, most internal organ–shifting roller coaster on the whole planet. According to the instructional safety video playing while we were waiting, the Shredder went up 435 feet into the sky, featured six loops, four corkscrews, and a heavy metal soundtrack blaring from the seat. That last part was to ensure that one way or another, your head would be aching by the time the ride ended. The impending negative g-force about to be splattered into my central nervous system was not something I was looking forward to.

"I'm terrified of heights and experience motion sickness more frequently than anyone I've ever known," I said. "Once, I used a moving walkway at the airport and had to sit down for an hour to regain my balance. You know, there are plenty of other rides here. Tamer ones. That merry-go-round looked like fun. Or the Haunted House? A nice walking tour like that can give us all the thrills we need."

Laura grabbed my shoulders and looked at me. "Don't wimp out now," she said. "We've been in line for an hour and a half. There are only a few more people in front of us. We're going on this ride, and it's going to be amazing." Her tone almost had me believing her for a second.

Then the cars that had just finished the ride pulled into the station. I counted no fewer than six people crying, and only three of them were children. A woman was shaking so much that her sunglasses had done a complete 180 on her head and were now perched precariously on her ears.

"Yeah, really amazing," I said.

The group in front of us was directed to the cars. Laura and I stepped forward. "All right, you're going to be in row one," the attendant said. "Please step down and to the right."

"Wait a minute," I said, feeling a bead of sweat trickle down my forehead. "Row one . . . you mean the *front* row?"

"No, we do things backward here," the attendant said, shaking his head. "What do you think, man? Yes, the front row. You're welcome. Now get going. We've got a long line."

I gulped. My feet were stuck to the cheap wooden boards beneath them. My brain kept saying, "*Move,*" but my feet simply didn't want to listen. I couldn't blame them; at this moment, they were the smartest part of me.

"Come on, let's go!" Laura said, grabbing my arm and scurrying down the loading platform. "This is gonna be so cool!"

It was around this time that I reconsidered my friendship with Laura. We'd known each other for about three years and had certainly had some memorable adventures—seeing concerts, driving across the country to visit national monuments, and even lazy Sunday brunches. Even better, there were never any romantic undertones when we hung out. There was no need to plan out a fancy move or play any games while communicating with each other. We were just our true, unfiltered selves. It was refreshing, and I really valued the time we spent together.

Anyway, I weighed if I wanted to throw that all away to avoid riding this roller coaster. It was really a fifty-fifty call.

I heard a *thunk* and looked down. Now I was sitting in my seat, the harness strapped over my shoulders. This was really happening. I looked at Laura. She was beaming. "Relax, you'll be fine," she said. Her enthusiasm was encouraging, but unfortunately wasn't infectious. I could already feel my stomach turning, and the heavy metal music hadn't even begun to play.

As soon as I had that thought, the music started blasting. It seemed like overkill to have dueling guitars chugging over an indistinguishable bass line and machine gun drums when we were still slowly easing out of the station. The car started climbing up the track, and an attendant waved goodbye to us. I wondered if her arm ever got tired from all the waving she had to do.

I leaned back in my seat and tried to relax. The coaster actually went up 509 feet, Laura told me, since the first big drop didn't take you all the way to the ground. So, I had nothing to do but listen to a heavy metal guy who sounded like he was dry heaving a complaint about the rising rates of healthcare or something. Strangely, it was calming my nerves.

Finally, we got to the point where I could have reached up and plucked a cloud out of the sky. They look so big up close! Ever since I was a kid, I thought it would be cool to hop up and down on a cloud. Of course, since they're not solid, that would be a terrible idea, but the thought of it is still fun. I looked over at Laura and feigned reaching up to a cloud. She smiled.

"You can almost grab one!" she yelled, barely audible over the heavy metal soundtrack. She was right. And that was a problem. I could actually move my arms quite a bit. In fact, I could move my *torso* back and forth, too. My hands shot up to the harness, which was no longer tightly protecting my shoulders, but instead appeared to be drifting away from the car entirely.

"Hey, Laura," I squeaked. "How does your harness feel?"

"Really tight!" she yelled back. "I can barely move at all!"

"Mine feels pretty loose," I said. "I'm a little concerned."

"Wait, what?" she yelled, as the train made its final ascent, and we paused for a moment at the top of the hill. "Stop messing around over there!"

In a flash, we were barreling down the drop of 435 majestic feet, and my harness was above my head. As my body jostled around the seat, I reached a hand up to try and pull the harness back down. Maybe if I gave it a really good tug, it would lock itself back into place. As soon as I yanked down though, the coaster shot into a corkscrew, and it took all the strength I could muster to fight gravity. There was a little crotch divider to keep your legs apart; I was clinging onto that like a nervous middle schooler clings onto the wall at a school dance.

Every time there was a straightaway, I thought it'd be a good time to reach up and pull down the harness. Unfortunately, each straight part of the track only lasted for a second and a half, tops, before we catapulted elsewhere on the ride. And every time, my butt flew even farther out of the seat. Five of the six loops and all of the corkscrews later, I was barely hanging on. My head was rattling, my stomach was lurching, and the heavy metal music only added to my anxiety.

The final loop came after another shot downhill. I leaned as far back in the seat as I could, as my harness was now permanently stuck in a nonworking position. The downhill part was no problem, and in fact was kind of peaceful. We passed by a boardwalk, where several people had congregated to watch the cars whizzing by. Did anyone notice I was mere seconds away from flying away into the abyss? Probably not. Nobody ever cares about someone else's problems.

As we went up into this last loop, my seat had finally had enough of me, and I was ejected from the car. Thinking quickly, I flung a hand out at whatever I could grab, which happened to be the harness. Thanks to the inversion, I was now grabbing one handle of the harness with my left hand, facing the oncoming cars. As the loop came and went, I didn't know if I was right side up or upside down. All I know is I was making direct eye contact with the kid in the seat behind me, and it was making him very uncomfortable.

I tried to display a calm demeanor, and despite the adrenaline rippling through my veins, I had to admit, the wind roaring through my hair provided a pleasant breeze. Perhaps if I had been securely relaxed on the seat instead of hanging on to the harness by three fingers, my entire body out of the car, I may have even found a moment of enjoyment during this ride. But any chance of that disappeared as soon as I ended up airborne.

I thought we were nearing the end of the ride, but when you're inverted, it's kind of difficult to keep track of time. Out of the corner of my eye, I saw a bunch of bright flashes go off. Boy, I'd love to see how *that* picture turned out.

My knuckles had turned a ghastly white from clutching onto the harness for what seemed like a good year and a half, but the train was finally starting to slow down. I swung my foot wildly in the air, eventually finding footing on the seat. I reached a hand to Laura, who grabbed it and held tight.

The train was crawling along at a snail's pace back to the station. I fell into the seat, my body forming a smear of sweat against the backrest. After what I had just been through, this was the most comfortable position I could get myself into.

With a horrible creak, the train mercifully ground to a halt. Everyone else's harnesses lifted up, and a joyous babble erupted from the other passengers as we exited the ride. "Oh my goodness, that was so much fun!" Laura exclaimed. "Did you have a good time?"

I looked at her. The world was still spinning around me. "Are you serious?" I asked her. "My harness flew up immediately. I was hanging on for dear life."

"What?" Laura said. "You seemed fine to me. You said the harness wasn't secure?"

"It was more than just insecure; it was like it wasn't there at all!" I shouted. How had she not noticed?

"Then we should tell someone about it."

"Good idea," I said, grabbing the sleeve of the attendant walking by. "Excuse me. There's a loose harness on that first car over there."

"On the train that's about to take off?" The attendant looked concerned.

"Yep, that's the one," I said.

The train had just started pulling out of the station. The attendant ran over to the ride's controls, slamming down his hand on the emergency stop button. The train promptly stopped as the passengers looked on with concern.

"We need to stop this train!" the attendant yelled. "There's something wrong with the harness in car one."

The attendant asked the people sitting in the front car to step out. He began poking around the seat, testing the harness in a number of ways, from pressing down on it with his hands to jumping with all of his weight on it. Finally, he walked over to where Laura and I were standing.

"Look, sir, I don't think that was very funny," he said. "There's nothing wrong with that harness, and because I hit the emergency stop button, we can't start things again until the maintenance team gets over here."

"But my harness really did fly up!" I said. "Ask my friend." I looked at Laura and she grimaced back at me.

"Honestly, I didn't see anything," she said. "Maybe you were exaggerating a bit? I know you get like that sometimes."

I did get like that sometimes, but this was no time for Laura to bring it up. How could she not have my back, after what we had just been through?

"Just like I thought," the attendant said. "Look, you two have to get out of here. This ride is closed for repairs now, anyway. Thanks a lot."

"That sucks. I was hoping to ride it a second time," Laura said. "I guess this is a good time to get lunch, then!"

I glared at her. The thought of lunch made my stomach turn all over again. We kept walking down the exit path and came to the photo kiosk. "Ooh, I want to see our photo!" Laura said, tugging at my shirt sleeve. "I was screaming that whole time. I bet it's so silly."

"Wait, this will show that I was hanging out of the harness!" I said. "We'll have to buy the photo, and then we can give it to the attendant. It'll show him I wasn't lying!"

"Okay, whatever you say," Laura said, offering me a polite smile. "Look, there we are!"

I looked up at the screen. There were two people that looked exactly like us on there, and Laura was right. She was screaming and looked ridiculous. And right next to her was me, looking like I had fainted in my seat. My eyes were closed, my mouth slightly agape, and my harness? Locked. Securely.

"Huh, guess you owe that attendant an apology after all," Laura said. I stared at the photo until it disappeared from the screen. Had I just imagined the whole thing? "Hey, at least you don't have to spend money on the photo," She did always see the positive in a situation. "Now let's go get some lunch, and we'll get back in line when the ride reopens!"

Just then, the ride whizzed by overhead. Laura and I looked up. I didn't get a great look at it, but I could have sworn I saw someone outside one of the cars, hanging on for dear life.

The Dude Who Hangs Out by the Bathroom at Parties

WHENEVER THERE'S A PARTY, THERE'S INEVITABLY GOING TO BE A long line for the bathroom. It doesn't matter if there are only four guests or four hundred. At some point, you'll find yourself in line with another person, forced to make chitchat.

For many people, this is their own kind of personal hell. For others, it's the best way to socialize. The Dude Who Hangs Out by the Bathroom at Parties falls into the latter category. He was a pretty social guy, and he knew there was one place where people couldn't resist going, especially at this party. Everyone was dressed up in costume, the salty snacks were plentiful, and the drinks were flowing. It was the perfect congruence of circumstances.

The Dude Who Hangs Out by the Bathroom at Parties decided to dress as Clint Eastwood from the movie *Gran Torino* tonight. His sweatpants—which may be the most comfortable piece of clothing on the entire planet—were high above his waist, nearly reaching his sternum. And his dark navy blue shirt did a fairly good job of hiding any sweat stains. Sometimes at parties, he got overheated, and the armpit waterworks started flowing. He had few methods for controlling it other than to wear dark clothing.

Hanging by the bathroom (naturally), The Dude Who Hangs Out by the Bathroom at Parties greeted a guest who walked up to the line. This guy wasn't dressed as anything, as far as the eye could tell.

"Some party, huh?" The Dude Who Hangs Out by the Bathroom at Parties said.

The guy stared blankly at him. "Why are your pants up so high?"

The Dude Who Hangs Out by the Bathroom at Parties laughed. "I'm Clint Eastwood from *Gran Torino*."

Over the next couple of minutes, the guy who wasn't dressed up as anything bad-mouthed the Clint Eastwood costume. The Dude Who Hangs Out by the Bathroom at Parties looked around nervously, hoping someone else would join the line. His wish was granted when a guy who was drumming all over his thighs stopped by. He was dressed like Carlton from *The Fresh Prince*, but he tried to explain that he was Steve from the children's show *Blue's Clues*, which seemed kind of strange for an adult party. But The Dude Who Hangs Out by the Bathroom at Parties was happy someone else was getting the brunt of the criticism. That is, until the guy dressed as Steve thought the costume of The Dude Who Hangs Out by the Bathroom at Parties was old John Travolta from *Saturday Night Fever*. Finally, the mean guy walked into the bathroom, and the guy dressed as Steve shrugged.

"Hey, if you were John Travolta, you could do some real fun dance moves."

He rocked his body for a bit, showing off some outrageous wiggling. It was a combination of the robot and the funky chicken, but with even less grace somehow. The Dude Who Hangs Out by the Bathroom at Parties was worried this guy might hurt himself.

"Hmm, you know, you may be right," The Dude Who Hangs Out by the Bathroom at Parties said. "I'll have to consider that for next time. But I gotta stick with Clint Eastwood tonight. Everyone already knows me as him! It'd be silly to change characters halfway through the party."

"Whatever you say, chief," Steve said, saluting as he kept dancing. "Hey, do you mind if I go to the bathroom ahead of you? There's this girl I'm talking to that I think is really into me!"

"Sure, go ahead," The Dude Who Hangs Out by the Bathroom at Parties said. "Just don't dance too much in there," he added, giving a playful elbow to Steve.

Steve stopped dancing. "Why would I do that? I'm only using the bathroom." His nose scrunched up, like he smelled something terrible. "Just let me go to the bathroom, okay?"

"Okay," The Dude Who Hangs Out by the Bathroom at Parties said, bothered by this sudden change in tone. "Have a good night."

With nobody else in line, The Dude Who Hangs Out by the Bathroom at Parties drifted back to the party. He did like to occasionally wander away from the bathroom, especially to go hang out by the snack bowls. There were no fewer than five bowls of chips—overwhelming to someone who wasn't a chip professional. The Dude Who Hangs Out by the Bathroom at Parties grabbed a chip from the red bowl, which looked the most promising, and moseyed on over to a corner.

A woman who had certainly had a drink or two came up to him. She looked like she was on a path of flirting destruction.

"Aren't those chips just amazing?" she said, her eyes wide with excitement.

"Yeah, they're pretty good!" The Dude Who Hangs Out by the Bathroom at Parties said. "I wish I had grabbed more than this one. But I didn't want to get too thirsty."

The woman threw her head back and laughed. "You're right! Chips really do make you thirsty, huh?"

"It's their trick. It's how they get you to order more drinks and other food at restaurants. You ever go into a Mexican place, and they keep bringing you chips? It's for a reason. It's to get you so thirsty and craving additional hydration that you order an extra drink or another dish. There's a science to it."

The woman was rubbing her chin, deep in thought. "That's absolutely fascinating," she said.

"Why thank you," The Dude Who Hangs Out by the Bathroom at Parties said. He gestured to her outfit. "May I guess who you're supposed to be?"

"Just don't say—*hiccup*—drunk!" she said. She threw her head back and laughed again. "I've only had one and a half vodka and soda waters."

"Ha, I wasn't going to guess that," The Dude Who Hangs Out by the Bathroom at Parties said. He flashed a smile. "You look a lot more radiant than a drunk woman."

"Aw, that's sweet," the woman said. She pointed at him. "Clint Eastwood, right?"

"That's right!" The Dude Who Hangs Out by the Bathroom at Parties said. His eyes lit up. "Nobody has gotten it right yet."

He was impressed with her eye for costumes, but after a few sentences he realized they didn't really have anything in common. Plus, vodka was his least favorite drink, and the smell of her cup as she waved it around was making him agitated. He quickly excused himself to head back to the bathroom.

"You hurry, now!" she called after him. "Oh, hello again, Steve from *Blue's Clues!*"

The Dude Who Hangs Out by the Bathroom at Parties was shocked to find a line of nine people waiting to use the bathroom. This was the biggest haul of the night!

He walked up to a gorgeous woman dressed as Marilyn Monroe. There was always one at every costume party. He opened his mouth to say hello, but before he could, he heard a voice behind him.

"Hey, asshole," the voice said. "You think you can just cut in line?"

The Dude Who Hangs Out by the Bathroom at Parties turned. A man in some kind of karate outfit was pointing his finger behind him. "This is where the line starts. You don't get to hop in front of everyone just because you're dressed like an unemployed loser."

"Oh, no," The Dude Who Hangs Out by the Bathroom at Parties said. "I was only coming to say hello. Of course I wouldn't cut in line."

"Yeah, yeah. Save it for someone who cares," the karate kid said. "How about you stop trying to be a hero and get to the back of the line. Everyone else is able to do it and wait patiently. You should do the same."

"But I'm just trying to—"

"Look, nobody wants to hear it!" the karate kid shouted. "There's one bathroom here, and we all have to wait our turns. That's first grade manners! Didn't you pass first grade?"

The Dude Who Hangs Out by the Bathroom at Parties looked toward the woman dressed as Marilyn Monroe, his eyes pleading for some sympathy. She shrugged. "Sorry," she said, her big blue eyes piercing into his soul. "But you did cut in line, and that's pretty rude."

The karate kid applauded. "See? Nobody's a fan of your antics."

The Dude Who Hangs Out by the Bathroom at Parties glared at him. He glumly walked back to the end of the line. "I'm Clint Eastwood, by the way," he said through clenched teeth.

"Not so lucky today, are you, punk?" the karate kid replied. He roared with laughter, and high-fived his friend who was in line with him. "Get it? Because that's one of his movies. And you're not lucky at all, because you tried to cut in line and instead got called out for your crap."

"Yes, I got it," said The Dude Who Hangs Out by the Bathroom at Parties. "And you're dressed as Kreese from *The Karate Kid*, right? Because you're an asshole?"

The rest of the line froze.

"What did you say to me?" the karate kid asked. "I must have misheard, because I know you didn't just call me an asshole."

He walked up to The Dude Who Hangs Out by the Bathroom at Parties, towering over him. The karate kid looked like he may have actually been a black belt. Either way, The Dude Who Hangs Out by the Bathroom at Parties didn't want to find out. "I didn't say anything," he said sullenly. "In fact, I was just leaving."

The Dude Who Hangs Out by the Bathroom at Parties headed toward the exit, peering over his shoulder to make sure the karate kid wasn't following him.

As he stepped out into the night, he realized he really did have to use the bathroom. He walked a few houses down, debating whether he should go back or try to quickly call a cab. But that moment of indecision caused him to teeter over the edge. He rapidly unzipped his pants, unleashing a stream of urine over the lawn. The Dude Who Hangs Out by the Bathroom at Parties wasn't proud of this moment, but he figured it was dark enough, and the moisture might be good for the grass.

As he was zipping up, a light flicked on over the front porch. A man in a robe and slippers started down the steps. "What are you doing?" the man said. "Get off my lawn!"

"Hey, that's my line," The Dude Who Hangs Out by the Bathroom at Parties said.

"What are you even talking about?" the man said. "Your line? Just get out of here. And try putting on some real clothes next time you leave the house. I was in bed and I still look more put together than you. A little bit of effort goes a long way." He turned the porch light off and closed the door.

The Dude Who Hangs Out by the Bathroom at Parties sighed. He made a promise to himself—no more costume parties.

The Principal's Office

"MR. WALTON WILL BE WITH YOU IN A MOMENT, MR. FINNEGAN. Please have a seat."

Louis Finnegan threw himself into the chair closest to the door. He was livid over being sent to the principal's office in the first place. All he had done was ask for a pizza party in Spanish class. Señora Malitez had promised the class a pizza party if the average class score on the last test was ninety percent or better. And what did they average on the last test? 89.6%! Louis wasn't a math whiz, but he knew you always rounded up in a situation like that. And by Señora Malitez's decree, that meant the class was going to get a pizza party.

The promise was made two weeks ago. Every day since then, a student had asked when the pizza party was going to happen. Louis had done it twice, sure, but so had his other classmates! Cat Womardia had asked, twirling her hair around her finger while she spoke in her singsong voice. Pat Jones didn't even really ask, but rather shouted "pizza party" for the final ten minutes of a class last week. Even Frederick Marquis, the French foreign exchange student who wanted to learn Spanish "to impress the ladies," had posed a pizza party *pregunta*. Wasn't French already the romantic language?

Despite all of these transgressions taking place, only Louis had gotten sent to the principal's office. And he wasn't happy about it at all. He had been here before, but it looked different this time. It was nearly winter break, and the decor reflected that. Of course, with political correctness on everyone's minds, the school couldn't outright say those were Christmas lights or a Hanukkah menorah. No, they were simply "holiday hues" and "a festive candelabrum."

There was a light hum of Bing Crosby over the office speakers, as well. Louis couldn't really make out the words, but figured Bing was singing one of his classics, like "Here Comes A Man with Presents" or "I'm Dreaming of a Colorless December."

What a joke, Louis thought to himself, seething quietly in the chair. Normally he was outspoken, but right now, his rage was silent. Nobody else was even aware it was going on, but if they were to interrupt the anger that simmered within, especially at the wrong moment, it certainly wouldn't end well.

"Mr. Finnegan?" a voice broke through the silence.

"What do you want!" Louis fired back.

"Uh, Mr. Walton will see you now."

"Oh," Louis said. He became slightly more tranquil as he stood up from his seat. "Thanks."

Louis had to hand it to Mr. Walton. He had somehow made the principal's office permanently smell like a museum. It was likely due to all of the figurines the principal picked up from various historical landmarks. Louis understood the desire for an Eiffel Tower doodad or a replica of the Sydney Opera House. Not nearly as comprehensible was a miniature IHOP from Alabama or a pair of legs standing on four squares, signifying the Four Corners of Colorado, Utah, New Mexico, and Arizona.

"Well, Mr. Finnegan." the principal began. "I see you're back here for another visit. I thought, after the last time, we wouldn't be crossing paths for a while. Please, have a seat."

"Well, Mr. Walton," Louis said. He leaned forward in his chair, drumming his fingers together right in front of his chin, mimicking the principal's mannerisms. He paused for dramatic effect, doing his best to collect his thoughts. "It appears I am back."

"Astute as ever, Mr. Finnegan," Mr. Walton said. "But the real question is *why*? Why are you back here again?"

"I asked for a pizza party in Spanish class," Louis said.

"Oh, come on now, Mr. Finnegan," Mr. Walton said, shaking his head. "I have the note right here. It says you were being insubordinate and using foul language. Enough with the lies!"

"I'm telling you the truth!" Louis said. "Señora Malitez promised us a pizza party if we got a high enough grade on our last test, and we did. So, we've been asking for one ever since, and today she sent me here. It's stupid, though. The entire class was asking for one. I don't know why she singled me out."

"Mr. Finnegan," Mr. Walton said, "need I remind you that it's against school policy for a teacher to offer such a blatant bribe to his or her students?"

"I'm not a teacher, so I didn't know that was a rule," Louis said. "Seems pretty stupid, though." Mr. Walton raised an eyebrow. *Don't say it's not a surprise*, Louis thought. "Not like it's much of a surprise, though. Your policies tend to follow a pattern of stupidity." *Thanks, big mouth.*

"Mr. Finnegan, I would not be pushing your luck if I were you. Remember who is in the position of power here."

"With all due respect, sir, there are a lot of things going on at this school that you should be concerned about," Louis said. "Which teachers are or are not giving pizza parties is among the least of your concerns. Or at least I sure hope so."

"Well, Mr. Finnegan, how about we call Señora Malitez in here to give her side of the story? Surely you did something beyond merely asking for pizza."

"Be my guest," Louis said. *Don't say anything about not getting back to class.* "Anything to stop me from getting back to class." *Dammit.*

"Luckily for you, class has ended, so I'll overlook that little comment." Mr. Walton said. He pushed a button on his desk. "Marlene, can you ring Señora Malitez for me, please?"

Marlene walked into the office. "Sir, I've told you. The intercom is broken. Just speak a little louder if you need me."

"Right," Mr. Walton said. "Please call Señora Malitez and have her come to the office. Let's see if Mr. Finnegan's story checks out."

ACCORDING TO SEÑORA MALITEZ, Louis raised his hand and said, "Profesora, cuándo vamos a tener la fiesta de pizza?" Getting pizza at school was one of the rare pleasures the students enjoyed. The cafeteria pizza rectangles simply weren't very tasty, so if a teacher ever went outside the school walls to bring in a pie or two, it was a dream scenario.

"Silencio, Louis," Señora Malitez said. "Ya no hables más."

"Pero usted prometió!" Louis said.

Señora Malitez picked up a piece of paper from her desk and walked up to where Louis was sitting. "Look, Mr. Finnegan, I know there's a rule about not using English in this class, but maybe something has gotten lost in translation here," she said, placing the paper on his desk. "I promised a pizza party if the class collectively averaged ninety percent on their last exam. And as this grade sheet shows, though the class gave a great effort and came very close, the average was only an 89.6%."

"But why wouldn't you round up?" Louis said. "Every other teacher does!"

"Because that's giving you something you didn't deserve," Señora Malitez said. "The real world is *difícil*, Mr. Finnegan. If you get handouts throughout your entire school year, you're only being set up to fail once you're out there."

"This is such a load of crap!" Louis said. A few other students began applauding his gall. "I think all you're doing is teaching us the real world is full of disappointment."

"Well, it seems you and I do agree on that point, Mr. Finnegan," Señora Malitez said, gazing wistfully out the window. She turned her head back to him. "But the fact remains that we will not be having a pizza party. That means you need to stop asking for one and disrupting the class. Everyone else here seems to be okay with no pizza party. Why does it mean so much to you?"

"But we've all been asking for it!" Louis said. "I'm not the only one."

"Look around you, Mr. Finnegan," Señora Malitez said, gesturing to the rest of the class. "They're all watching you cause a scene. They're not improving their participles or gerunds at all. I had plans to teach the class new ways to use the future tense, but now that's a thing of the past. You really must let this pizza party fantasy go."

"It's not even the pizza party itself," Louis said. "It's that you broke a promise to the class."

"Okay, I don't know what else to tell you," Señora Malitez said. She sounded exasperated. "It's not happening."

The five-minute warning bell echoed throughout the classroom. Señora Malitez looked up at the clock.

"Already? How?" she muttered. She turned back toward Louis. "That's it, Mr. Finnegan. You're going to the principal's office."

"AND THAT'S HOW IT HAPPENED!" Louis said. "Is that really worthy of detention?"

"Sounds to me like you were making a scene in class," Mr. Walton said. "Señora Malitez was just trying to further everyone's education, and you kept interrupting. You know our policy on causing a ruckus."

"Yeah, another dumbass policy of yours," Louis replied. He mentally smacked the side of his head.

"I suppose we shouldn't be so surprised," Señora Malitez said. "Mr. Finnegan is nearly flunking my class, after all."

"I just got an A on your last test!" Louis said. "And I got an A on the one before that! How could I be flunking?!"

"Unfortunately, Mr. Finnegan, test scores are not the only component of your final grade in my course," Señora Malitez said. "Behavior plays a big part as well. And being sent to the principal's office so often is certainly not doing you any favors."

"You've sent me here once!" Louis said. "Today! Right now! How does that turn my grade into an F?"

"Mr. Finnegan, there's no need to raise your voice," Señora Malitez said. "Perhaps if you applied yourself more diligently and stopped acting out in class, you wouldn't be in this predicament in the first place."

"Perhaps Mr. Finnegan needs a stricter form of punishment than simply visiting my office," Mr. Walton said. "Say . . . three weeks detention?"

"Really? Three weeks detention because I asked about pizza." Louis was stunned. Surely this had to be some kind of joke.

"It's more of a general insubordination punishment," Mr. Walton said. "From the sound of it, you've been speaking out in class, cursing, pushing fellow students out of their seats, and being a disruption toward the learning environment."

Don't say this is bullshit. Don't say it. "Man, this is bullshit!" Louis said. *Once again, big mouth, you've dug your own grave.*

"Well, Mr. Finnegan, since you're so opposed to following the rules of authority, why don't we make it an even month of detention?" Mr. Walton leaned in, challenging Louis to say something else. "Do I make myself clear?"

Louis sighed heavily, hunching his shoulders and gazing down at the floor. There was no use trying to reason with them anymore. As he had discovered all too often during his high school years, he couldn't win. "Yes, sir."

"Good. We'll escort you over there," Mr. Walton said.

Detention was held in one of the school's largest classrooms, a former science lab converted into a small lecture hall. It could hold around a hundred students and, perhaps by design, was right across the hall from the teacher's lounge. Louis imagined someone keeping watch through the window to make sure no one tried to escape the detention room.

"Wait, do you guys smell that?" Louis said. He stopped just in front of the detention hall door. "Is . . . is that pizza?"

Louis swung open the door, his face beaming with excitement. He peered inside the room but only saw a smattering of students and the detention attendant.

"Mr. Finnegan, it appears your nose is playing tricks on you," Mr. Walton said, chuckling softly. "We don't offer any food in detention. Now go on and get in there."

Mr. Walton turned toward the teacher's lounge, grabbing the door for Señora Malitez. As he opened it up, the smell of pizza intensified.

Louis took a few steps toward the teacher's lounge. He spotted a stack of pizza boxes on a table. All of his teachers were inside, munching on slices. He saw Mr. Patterstone enjoying a slice of pepperoni. Miss Gregory was gingerly nibbling on a piece of veggie. Even Mrs. Lonnie, the stern biology teacher who Louis had never once seen smile, was chatting and laughing with her fellow teachers, swinging a slice of pizza around as she gestured wildly.

"Wait a minute—*you're* all having a pizza party?" Louis said. "You sonsabitches! The whole lot of you! Sonsabitches!"

The teachers in the lounge stopped talking and laughing and all turned and stared at Louis. Mr. Walton leaned down to him.

"Now, Mr. Finnegan, what did we say about using that kind of language?" he whispered. He was barely audible, but Louis could sense the tension in his voice.

"Yeah, but this is some real crap here," Louis said. "It's like you're rubbing it in my face."

"Well, that would be a waste of good pizza, wouldn't it?" Mr. Walton said. "Now get over there. Oh, and make yourself comfortable. That little outburst just earned you detention for the rest of the school year."

The principal closed the door, leaving Louis to stand sadly in the hallway. He turned and walked into the detention hall, grabbing a seat in the back row. He flung his backpack on the table and settled into his chair. After a minute, the kid next to him tapped him on the shoulder.

"What are you in here for?" he asked. "I burned a hole on the science lab table by pouring a beaker of acid on it."

"I asked for a pizza party in Spanish class and got sent here," Louis said. "Then things, uh, escalated a little bit."

"Oh man, that's rough!" the kid replied. "Seems like a pretty stupid reason for a detention."

"Yeah, you're telling me," Louis said. "But I guess I'll be in here awhile, so better get used to it."

"It's not so bad," the kid said. "And hey, maybe you'll even get some pizza after all. They brought some in yesterday. I think it was maybe left over from a teacher's birthday celebration or something. It was such a nice surprise!"

"Wait, you mean you had a pizza party in detention?" Louis asked.

"Ha, yeah, I guess we did!" the kid said. "Man, too bad you didn't get sent here yesterday."

Just Don't Forget About Me

SIMON GAZED OUT INTO THE WILDERNESS BEFORE HIM. PEOPLE often told him he saw things in two dimensions, but he disagreed. The world was a big, unlimited place, and he wanted to explore every crevice of it.

Today, he was standing on the edge of a canyon, surveying the land out in front of him. The sky was shining a gorgeous shade of blue, with nary a cloud staining it. Off in the distance, a trio of bountiful trees sprouted up from the ground. In the bright sun, the canyon itself seemed even more vibrant than usual, a cool tan instead of its more standard shade of muddy brown.

Yes, today was a very good day. Simon glanced back and noticed his dog, Roscoe, coming toward him. Roscoe seemed to have unlimited energy, sometimes bounding through the air toward Simon. He was a good pup. Roscoe was a mutt, for sure, but if Simon had to take a stab at his dog's lineage, he'd guess there was a mix of golden retriever, dachshund, and French bulldog.

It was a pretty ridiculous combination, but then again, Roscoe was a pretty ridiculous dog. His tongue often came out of his mouth, flailing in all kinds of crazy directions. Sometimes his fur stuck straight up off his back, too. It was like he couldn't decide what kind of hair day to have, so he just said, "Forget it" and went wild.

Before Roscoe could get over to where Simon was standing, a few new people joined the scene. Simon had never seen these people before, and he wasn't sure if he liked their type. From what he could make out, there were four people coming along—three women and one man.

The first woman was a bit of a strawberry blonde, with a long red shirt that essentially served as a dress. She may have had shorts on, though Simon couldn't see any. He wasn't sure when this trend of shirtdresses started, but he believed it had to stop immediately.

Next to Miss Shirtdress was another woman wearing a red shirt, though she had on black pants. That seemed excessively hot with the sun shining so brightly, but she appeared comfortable enough. Her hair spiraled upward in a blonde beehive, harkening back to the 1950s, when women could have hairstyles that weighed twenty pounds but somehow didn't affect their gait or posture at all. She was gesticulating wildly with her left arm. She must have been very excited to get to the edge of the canyon.

A very sunburned gentleman was keeping pace just behind the two ladies. His burgundy skin made his green eyes protrude even more noticeably from his head. They were so bulbous, they looked nearly frog-like, and Simon wondered if the man also had a tongue that liked to snatch flies out of the air. He guessed yes. The man's faded blue jeans and loud Hawaiian shirt only furthered Simon's belief that the man got sunburned from falling asleep next to a pool at a hotel, perhaps while sipping on a strawberry daiquiri or some other sugary drink.

Accompanying Mr. Sunburn was a woman who looked absolutely ghostly by comparison. Simon just assumed her skin was naturally pale but being next to an increasingly florid man really highlighted the difference. She was wearing a tight purple dress, with one leg noticeably longer than the other. Simon wondered if that slowed her down at all, particularly while she was running. Her hair stuck out in all directions, like a box of French fries being featured photographically on a fast food menu.

Simon wasn't sure he wanted to find out who these people were. They looked like an erratic bunch, and he wasn't feeling particularly sociable at the moment. He simply wanted to gaze over the abyss with Roscoe perched loyally by his side. That didn't seem to be asking too much.

Simon's eyes drifted back over the canyon as he gazed out at the gorgeous beauty before him. The vast landscape was a good distraction from the approaching people, and he settled into the grass, giving Roscoe a good scratch.

He heard a scream behind him. They had been standing near the edge of the canyon—had one of them fallen in?

Simon and Roscoe hustled over to where the people stood. He no longer saw Miss Shirtdress. He peered over the edge, seeing if he could catch a glimpse of her down below. No sign of anyone.

Simon brought his head back from over the edge. Now Mr. Sunburn and Miss Purple Dress were both gone, too. Simon looked in confusion at Ms. Black Pants. She pointed behind him. The trees that were off in the distance had been replaced by a cactus that was way too big. It was crooked and seemed to be poking the sun. What in the world was going on?

When Simon turned back around, the last woman was gone. She was right there! Had she gone off to look for the others? She should have told him if that was her plan. He shrugged. Oh, well. Just the two of them would be more fun, anyway.

He turned to Roscoe, but he wasn't there anymore, either. Now Simon was really worried. He peered over the edge of the canyon.

Surely Roscoe hadn't jumped down; he was afraid of heights. He hesitated to even get near the ledge when Simon had been looking for the other people. No, he must have gone off to find some grass or something. He sure did love rolling around in a freshly cut field.

While Simon was looking around for his trusty dog, he sensed a darkness approaching even before the sky became overcast above him. He felt the hair on the back of his neck stand up. He tilted his head back and looked up at what was causing the darkness. It appeared to be a big, pink, round object, like a piece of bubblegum that had just been unwrapped. Or maybe some kind of ball?

Simon had never seen anything like this before. The blob appeared to be connected to something silver above it, with a larger yellowish protuberance on the other end, though Simon couldn't quite make out what it was. He looked around again for Roscoe, but still, no sign of him.

The pink ball was drawing closer. Simon figured he probably shouldn't be in its way and tried to walk back away from the canyon. Only his legs weren't working. His feet were stuck to the ground, refusing to budge. Simon looked down and, in horror, saw his feet were pointing in opposite directions.

Simon looked back up. The pink ball had nearly enveloped him. He threw his arms up to hold it back, but it was too late. The pink ball struck him in the abdomen, a blow to the stomach that he had never felt before and never wanted to feel again. The pink ball gyrated—first to the left, then to the right.

As it continued this uncoordinated dance, Simon realized he could no longer feel his legs. He looked down at where they once had been and now saw absolutely nothing. Only a few scraps of pink residue lay before him. Where had his legs gone?

The pink ball hurled itself at Simon and grazed his cheek. He tried to hold a hand up to his face, but there was nothing to move to gauge the veracity of his fresh wound. Incredulous, Simon's mouth formed an "O" shape as, with one final blow, the pink ball took away his vision. In an instant, he had been reduced to a small, obscure speck.

Simon's mind was racing. Where was he? Why couldn't he move? Why couldn't he see? Where was Roscoe? He just wanted to feel again.

Simon spent what seemed like an eternity in a sort of limbo, not quite sure what was going on. As he was just about to give up hope, Simon's eyes fluttered open. He yelped in excitement. Looking down, he saw the rest of him starting to come back. First his torso, then his arms and legs, and finally his feet. And they were pointing in the right direction!

Simon walked over to the field of grass nearby and laid down in it. As he was looking up at the now completely red sky, he felt a tongue on his cheek. It was Roscoe, coming to check on his old pal. Simon hugged Roscoe. They were reunited again and celebrated by rolling around on the grass until they grew tired.

Stubbed Tow

"HAVE A NICE DAY, SIR."

"Go screw yourself."

Marcie smiled. She had been working at Oscar & Koch Towing Company for about two years now, and she considered herself one of the lucky few that actually loved her job. She looked forward to coming to work each day. Her friends thought she was crazy. She couldn't possibly enjoy working for a towing company, they'd say. Marcie just shook her head and told them they didn't understand.

Of course, nobody likes being towed. There's no great situation for having a truck come and take your car. Consider the possibilities: Either you're parked illegally somewhere, or your car has broken down and needs repairs. That's really about it. Neither one of those circumstances screams "good time."

Sometimes, the illegality of your parking didn't even have to be obvious. For Marcie, those were the truly fun cases. O&K Towing was known for getting those fringe parkers. The type that tried to squeeze into a tight spot on the street and have an inch of bumper sticking into the red "No Parking" area. Or perhaps they weren't the proper distance away from a fire hydrant. Or maybe they pulled into a friend's apartment complex late one night and parked in the spot next to visitor's parking, even though six of the eight spots in the row were totally fine for visitors to park in, and there was no signage indicating which spots were which.

Marcie loved those people most of all, because they were the most miserable. There was something satisfying about bringing people down to her level. One of those people was approaching. A harried woman was storming up to the counter. Marcie guessed she was the type of woman who couldn't put lipstick on without getting the majority of it on her teeth.

"Where is my car?" the woman yelled. "I was just visiting my friend for dinner at her apartment. She lives in a closed community! You assholes really have nothing better to do than tow people who are only trying to eat? Are you that depressed?"

Marcie enjoyed these angry customers. They were so much easier to toy with. "I'm sorry to hear that, ma'am," she said, her lips curled into her best fake smile. "But we only tow in areas with clearly marked signs. It's the driver's responsibility to know the legality of a parking spot."

"Are you kidding me?" the woman said. "There's *one* tiny sign at the entrance, tucked under a tree. You have to nearly hop the curb to see it. And there's no notice throughout the community at all. There wasn't even anyone else parked around me; it's not like I was blocking anyone else from parking. You assholes are just taking advantage of innocent people."

"It seems like everyone else knew that area was a no-parking zone," Marcie said. "After all, you said you were the only one parked there, right?"

"You bitch," the woman snarled. "You're a joke. Just let me get my car, okay?"

"I can't just *let* you have it," Marcie said, making a big gesture with her hand for emphasis. "The cost is two hundred and forty dollars."

"You cannot be serious," the woman said. "What does that pay for?"

"It pays for your car," Marcie said. "And that is what you said you wanted, yes?"

Marcie knew this woman was at her wit's end, and she loved it. The actual cost of the tow in this situation would be no more than one hundred and fifty dollars, but Marcie was hoping to pocket the extra cash.

"You know it is, you asshole," the woman said. "I want to know why it's so damn expensive."

"It's standard towing fare," Marcie said. "Unfortunately, our card machine is experiencing some technical difficulties. It'll take up to one hundred and fifty dollars, but the rest will have to be in cash."

"Of course," the woman said. "You can't even get your credit card machine sorted out. You've screwed me over on everything else. Why would this be any different?" She pulled out a card and a wad of cash from her purse.

"Glad you understand," Marcie said, taking the card and cash from the woman. "I'll be back in a moment."

Marcie disappeared from the window. She went to the back room and studied the vending machine. It was still a couple of hours until her lunch break, so she wanted to grab a snack. But she was torn between chocolate and candy. Maybe a Twix would satisfy her craving. Caramel never let her down.

Marcie slid seventy-five cents into the machine and hit D-5. Two Twix fell out into the drawer. Marcie smiled at her luck. *One for now, one for later*, she thought.

She opened up the first package and pulled out one of the Twix. She munched a few bites before returning to the window, the Twix still in her hand. "I'm sorry, which car is yours?"

The woman erupted into a volley of profanities, each one more vulgar and obscure than the last. Marcie continued nibbling on her Twix, nodding every once in a while. A crumb fell from her lips onto the counter. "Are you even listening?" the woman screeched. A bright blue vein on her forehead had started pulsing. Marcie wondered if her head might actually explode. She hoped not; it would be an absolute mess to clean up.

"Just give me my car," the woman continued, shaking her head. "It's the red Camry. Okay?"

"Right away, ma'am," Marcie said. She proceeded to do her best impression of a tortoise as she sauntered over to the computer. She typed on a few of the keys and banged the space bar six times for emphasis. She had finished the Twix, and the satisfaction in her stomach was enough to let this woman finally get her car. That, plus the extra ninety dollars Marcie had pocketed. She came back to the window. "All right, ma'am, you can go out and get your car. I'll open the gate just enough for you to drive through."

"About damn time," the woman said. "You're horrible. Hope you have an awful day."

"That's sweet of you to say," Marcie said. "Drive safe!"

The woman slammed the door behind her as she left the office. When she arrived at the gate, Marcie made a big show of opening it, acting as if the task were the most difficult thing in the world to do. The woman drove through the small opening, nearly ripping through the fencing.

Marcie chuckled to herself. What fun! As she returned to the office, she encountered a man who looked exactly like her ex-boyfriend.

"Hi there," he said, in a surprisingly sweet tone. "Do you have my car? It's a '14 Ford Fusion."

The computer notes said he had parked in a school zone for three minutes while he got his son. O&K Towing didn't care, though; the tow truck swooped in and snatched up his car like an eagle plucking a fish out of the sea. Marcie smiled her little smile. It had become habitual at this point. She liked how it signified, "I'm here to help you, but I'm going to make sure you really earn it."

"We've got a few Ford Fusions in here," she said, looking back toward the lot. "Do you know what color it is?"

"Ah, it's some kind of gray," he said, scratching the back of his head. "I think they call it 'charcoal,' officially."

"You'll have to be more specific than that, sir," Marcie said, continuing to smile. "Seems like everyone has a gray car these days."

The man peered into the lot. There were a handful of gray cars, but for the most part, it was a colorful bunch.

"I think I see it over there, actually," he said, pointing to the third row. "It's next to that red truck."

"Unfortunately, I can't just have you walk in and take any car you choose," Marcie said. Her ex would do something like that. He always had to pick the movie they watched or the game they played.

"That's not at all what I'm trying to do," the man said.

"Look, do you want your car or not?"

The guy nodded. "I think it's pretty obvious that I do," he said. "Maybe if I give you my license plate number? Will that do it?" His tone had lost its initial sweetness. Marcie loved draining whatever happiness a person had when they came to the lot.

She shook her head. "Sorry, but the computer is down today, so I wouldn't be able to look up your car by its license plate number."

The man sighed. He rubbed his forehead a bit. "Okay, that's certainly not helpful. . . . How about if I say the license plate number, and you can go check the lot for the car? I can see it from here. That will only take a few minutes."

"Sure, and then I suppose you'll just take my stuff and never give it back," Marcie said. That was something else her ex did. This guy was just like him.

"Look, I don't know what all you're dealing with here," the man said, his voice rising with anger. "But I'm only trying to get my car."

"Just shut up," Marcie said. "Let me think for a moment."

She tapped her pen on the desk in front of her. She could easily take this man to his car, but she was enjoying driving him crazy. Her eyes focused a little past his ears, making it seem like she was deep in thought.

"Okay, tell you what," she said, after a long pause. "I want to believe you. I really do. So, here's what I'll do for you. If you slip me an extra forty dollars, I'll take you to your car."

"Are you kidding me?" the man said, stepping away from the window counter. "You're really blackmailing me to get my car? That's unbelievable."

"It's hardly blackmail," Marcie said, feigning outrage at the mere suggestion. "I'm simply giving you an alternative so that you can go home with your car today. If you'd rather come back another time, I can certainly make a note of that as well, and you can be on your way."

"No, no . . . I already told my son to wait at the library until I could pick him up. I'll pay the stupid blackmail." The man was seething. "How much is it total?"

"For the car, $256. Forty more for me to take you there. And that part has to be in cash," Marcie said. She couldn't have this little tip going on the books.

The man reached into his wallet. "Here," he muttered, tossing a credit card at Marcie before pulling out two twenty-dollar bills. "Card for the tow, and forty for your blackmail."

"For my services, you mean," Marcie said. She didn't appreciate being called a blackmailer. She briefly considered closing the window and not taking the man to his car at all, but she had just made an extra forty dollars for being irritating. She didn't want to press her luck. "One moment, please."

Marcie disappeared from the window. She relished the fact that the window was uncomfortably low, so that visitors had to crouch down in order to talk to her. It made her feel like they were bowing before her throne.

When the computer was working normally—which included today, Marcie just felt like having a little fun—the process of running someone's plates and allowing them to go get their car would take about two minutes, maybe three if the internet was slow. But Marcie liked to make them wait. She'd often leave the room for upward of fifteen minutes, seeing how long she could disappear before they snapped. It usually wasn't very long.

Finally, when she decided her latest victim had had enough, she came back to the window. "All right, sir," she said, gesturing toward the lot. "I can't actually take you to your car, in case another customer comes. But go on through that door there, and get your car and come out to the gate. I'll open it up for you when you arrive."

The man snatched his keys out of her hand. "The only thing I want right now—the only thing that would make me truly happy," the man said, "would be to get away from you."

The man marched off, and Marcie froze. That was what her ex-boyfriend had said when he broke up with her. She saw a future for them together, and he wanted nothing to do with her. And now this doppelgänger was bringing up the past.

After letting the Fusion through the gate, Marcie stumbled back to her post at the window, just in time to see her coworker Mitch arrive to take over for her. "How are things going today?" Mitch asked.

"Huh?" Marcie replied, still thinking about her ex. "Oh, I guess it's okay. Lots of people. You know how it goes."

"Sure do," Mitch said. "Have a good night!"

Marcie hopped into her car and drove off. She muttered to herself the entire way home, fuming over what her ex's look-alike had said. How could that man have said that? Didn't he know how hurtful it was?

Marcie parked near her house. She hated how none of the homes in her area had garages, or even driveways. Street parking really was the only option. She hadn't spent a lot of time parallel parking while learning how to drive, and it always made for an interesting adventure when she tried to wedge herself in between two other cars. But tonight she handled the situation with style, easily gliding in between the cars that now sandwiched hers. Marcie nodded to herself, a wry smile crossing her lips. That made her feel a little bit better, at least.

The next morning, Marcie got up and got ready for work. When she stepped outside, her car was gone. She glanced up at the street sign next to the now vacant spot. It read, "Street Sweeping: 8 to 10 a.m."

"HEY THERE, WHAT CAN I DO YOU FOR?"

An overly enthusiastic man with a name tag that read "Craig" came out from behind the counter to greet Marcie. She had been towed by Cousins and Sons, the rival towing company across town. This was Marcie's first time being towed, and she wasn't sure she would enjoy being on the other side of things.

"I'm here to pick up my car," Marcie said. "It got towed this morning during street sweeping hours."

"Ah, yes, I remember that one coming in here," Craig said. "Real beautiful ride you got yourself there, missy!"

Marcie looked perplexed. No one had ever complimented her car before. She liked driving it around, so it was comforting to hear someone else praise it for a change.

"Yeah, I know," Marcie said. "About time it got some respect."

"The respect it deserves," Craig said. "Now, let's get you taken care of."

"Okay, do you think this will take very long?"

"Not at all—I'd say we'll have you out of here in about two minutes," Craig said. "I just want to go over your options. Now, the city has a fixed price for street sweeping fines, but since this is your first offense it'll be discounted."

"Wait, is that true?" Marcie asked. She had never heard of such a discount.

"It sure is!" Craig replied. "In fact, it's one of the first things they taught me when I started. We believe in looking out for our fellow drivers, so we're always trying to find ways to help people. Knowing the rules of the road and the city is a great place to start!"

"Yeah, I suppose it is," Marcie said.

"Now, you can either pay that fine all upfront now or in installments over the next six months if that'd be easier for you," Craig said. "Most places don't offer that choice, but we know how painful a tow can be, so we try to be flexible. If it's better for you to spread it out, we're happy to do it."

"Wow, that would actually be much better," Marcie said. She had spent most of her last paycheck on a new watch for her ex-boyfriend, just a day before he had broken up with her. Outside of the cash she had pocketed at work, she barely had a dime.

"Well then, let's get that going and get you all checked out of here," Craig said. "That'll just be fourteen dollars today, and if you're paying by card, we can set it up as a recurring for the next six months."

Marcie handed over her credit card. The man typed in her information and had her checked out within a few seconds. Marcie was impressed; even on the rare times she gave effort, she still couldn't get someone checked out this quickly.

"Okay, you're good to go," Craig said. "And keep an eye out for those street sweeping signs. They're tricky ones! Always take a look around before you leave the vehicle to make sure you're not missing anything."

Invigorated, Marcie grabbed her keys and got into her car. Maybe getting towed didn't have to be such a terrible experience after all. She looked in her rearview mirror and watched Cousins and Sons disappear in the distance. Yes, Craig had inspired Marcie to try being nice to people today.

At least to the people who were nice to her first.

The Last Donut

FROM: Jake Owens (j.owens@mildmanneredco.com)
TO: All 12th Floor (all@mildmanneredco.com)
SUBJECT: The Last Donut
TIME: 9:14 a.m.

Morning, everyone. Hope you all had a great weekend. Let's get down to business—I had a box of donuts in the kitchen. They clearly had my name written on them, and there were still four remaining when I left the office Friday night.

You can imagine my surprise when, stopping in the kitchen on my way in, all of the donuts were gone. Yet the empty box remained, making me think someone here took them. I'm not mad. I'd just like to know who did it, so you can buy me a donut sometime.

Thanks in advance,
Jake

FROM: Shaun Bennett (s.bennett@mildmanneredco.com)
TO: Jake Owens (j.owens@mildmanneredco.com)
SUBJECT: Re: The Last Donut
TIME: 9:17 a.m.

Jakeyyyy,

What's happening, man? Sorry to hear about the donut. I'm not point-ing any fingers, but I saw Brad from Accounting and he had a few crumbs around his mouth. May have been from a breakfast burrito or a croissant—also may have been from a donut. I don't want to put the blame on anyone but I'd ask him if I were you. Good luck, man.

Shaun

FROM: Jake Owens (j.owens@mildmanneredco.com)
TO: Brad Benjamin (b.benjamin@mildmanneredco.com)
SUBJECT: Re: The Last Donut
TIME: 9:20 a.m.

Hey Brad,

I'm sure you've seen my email by now, the one about the donuts. I understand you've taken one or maybe all of them from the box. Prob-ably a simple miscommunication, but they were actually my donuts.

If you could let me know it was you who did that, we can put this whole thing behind us and move on. We'll go grab a few donuts sometime. Your treat.

Thanks,
Jake

FROM: Brad Benjamin (b.benjamin@mildmanneredco.com)
TO: Jake Owens (j.owens@mildmanneredco.com)
SUBJECT: Re: The Last Donut
TIME: 9:24 a.m.

Hi Jake,

This is a rather perturbing email to receive, as I don't believe we've ever actually met. While the contents of my breakfast shouldn't concern you in the slightest, I was eating a sausage and egg sandwich from the bakery down the street. I believe they sell donuts as well. You could stop by there for one or two. I've tried a couple—they're quite tasty!

Best of luck,
Brad

FROM: Mindy Delvecchio (m.delvecchio@mildmanneredco.com)
TO: Jake Owens (j.owens@mildmanneredco.com)
SUBJECT: Re: The Last Donut
TIME: 9:25 a.m.

Jake,

Those donuts were yours? I saw them on Friday and was wondering who they belonged to. I didn't see your name on them at all, so I'm not sure whoever took them knew they were yours. Probably just an innocent mistake. We're still on for our call with the client in five minutes, right? I'm at home, waiting for the maintenance guy, but I'll dial in.

Talk to you then,
Mindy

FROM: Jake Owens (j.owens@mildmanneredco.com)
TO: Mindy Delvecchio (m.delvecchio@mildmanneredco.com)
SUBJECT: Re: The Last Donut
TIME: 9:26 a.m.

Yes, I'll be on. Just as soon as I figure out the culprit.

FROM: Derrick Porter (d.porter@mildmanneredco.com)
TO: Jake Owens (j.owens@mildmanneredco.com)
SUBJECT: Re: The Last Donut
TIME: 9:27 a.m.

Jake,

First of all, you're aware that we start at 8:30, right? Your message made it seem like you just got here and found the donuts missing.

Second, this is a gross misuse of company email. You know Mondays are already busy, and now you've got people concerned about donuts? They wouldn't even be good, anyway. Three days old . . . why are you so upset? Is everything okay at home?

You know my door's always open. Feel free to come chat if you need me.

Derrick

FROM: Cassidy Alvarez (c.alvarez@mildmanneredco.com)
TO: Mariah Lane (m.lane@mildmanneredco.com)
SUBJECT: Re: The Last Donut
TIME: 9:29 a.m.

Holy shit, does Jake not know he emailed that to the entire company?

Even Mr. Porter saw it! How can you not know what you're doing? Donuts aren't worth that!

By the way, how'd you like yours? I thought mine had really good frosting, and I always love some sprinkles, but it had a little bit of a weird aftertaste.

FROM: Mariah Lane (m.lane@mildmanneredco.com)
TO: Cassidy Alvarez (c.alvarez@mildmanneredco.com)
SUBJECT: Re: The Last Donut
TIME: 9:30 a.m.

You know Jake. He gets obsessed over the smallest things. He chewed me out once for putting a spoon into the sink instead of the dishwasher. If everything isn't just so, he goes nuts. Speaking of which, my donut had little chopped up peanuts on it. I liked it, but thought it smelled a little lemony, which was weird because I don't think any of those donuts were lemon-flavored? Maybe that smell was just lingering from the others. Either way, we should go get some more sometime! I'd love to see what they're like just out of the oven.

FROM: Jake Owens (j.owens@mildmanneredco.com)
TO: Brad Benjamin (b.benjamin@mildmanneredco.com)
SUBJECT: Re: The Last Donut
TIME: 9:36 a.m.

Brad,

I'm sorry to accuse you of taking the donuts, but I've asked around the office, and I can't help but think you're the guilty culprit. You did have crumbs on your lips this morning after all. I have it on good authority.

Again, while I'm disappointed, I won't be mad if you just come clean. It's much appreciated, and we'll forgive and forget over another dozen or two.

Thanks,
Jake

FROM: Brad Benjamin (b.benjamin@mildmanneredco.com)
TO: Jake Owens (j.owens@mildmanneredco.com)
SUBJECT: Re: The Last Donut
TIME: 9:40 a.m.

Jake, this is the last response I'm going to give you. I didn't take your donuts. I don't even work in the same building as you. Why would I go out of my way to grab a donut, especially when our landlord brings us fresh donuts every Monday anyway? I've actually eaten so many in the past few weeks that I made an active effort *not* to have any today.

I'm no therapist, but it seems like there's something bigger at play here than simply a few donuts. Mr. Porter is an empathetic man. Maybe go stop by his office to chat. It can only help.

Best of luck,
Brad

FROM: Mindy Delvecchio (m.delvecchio@mildmanneredco.com)
TO: Jake Owens (j.owens@mildmanneredco.com)
SUBJECT: Re: The Last Donut
TIME: 9:42 a.m.

Hi Jake,

Are you going to hop on this call? The client and I are both waiting for you. We don't have time to fool around like this. Worry about your donuts later.

Thanks,
Mindy

FROM: Derrick Porter (d.porter@mildmanneredco.com)
TO: Jake Owens (j.owens@mildmanneredco.com)
SUBJECT: Re: The Last Donut
TIME: 9:43 a.m.

Hi Jake,

I just got an angry email from Mudspray, wondering where you were. You and Mindy have a 9:30 call with them. She's on the line, but you're nowhere to be found.

You're not still upset over the donuts, are you? I told you, they're not even fresh anymore. Whoever ate them probably thought they were a little stale. You wouldn't have enjoyed them as much as you did last week.

I'll be back from an in-person at noon. Why don't you come to my office around then and we can talk? I think it'll do you good. I can even bring donuts.

Best,
Derrick

FROM: Mindy Delvecchio (m.delvecchio@mildmanneredco.com)
TO: Jake Owens (j.owens@mildmanneredco.com)
SUBJECT: Re: The Last Donut
TIME: 10:26 a.m.

Hey Jake,

Don't bother getting on the line. I handled the call myself. That was completely unprofessional hanging me out to dry like that, though. I'm new on this account, and you've been working with them for years.

It's okay, though. The client said he liked the way I operated, and he actually asked if I'd be his contact going forward. Hope you don't mind, but I'm going to take the lead on this account from now on.

Regards,
Mindy

FROM: Jake Owens (j.owens@mildmanneredco.com)
TO: Mindy Delvecchio (m.delvecchio@mildmanneredco.com)
SUBJECT: Re: The Last Donut
TIME: 10:32 a.m.

Sounds great, I didn't really like that client very much anyway. I'll let you know on the status of the donuts—I've got a good lead cooking.

Jake

FROM: Derrick Porter (d.porter@mildmanneredco.com)
TO: Jake Owens (j.owens@mildmanneredco.com)
SUBJECT: Re: The Last Donut
TIME: 12:15 p.m.

Hi Jake,

Sorry I'm a bit late in getting back to my office, but I'll be here the rest of the day. Please pop by when you get a chance. I'd like to just chat about how things are going. And you're going to love this—I got a dozen donuts from that shop down the street. Okay, I snuck one, but there still are eleven left. And that one I had was delicious!

See you soon,
Derrick

FROM: Jake Owens (j.owens@mildmanneredco.com)
TO: Derrick Porter (d.porter@mildmanneredco.com)
SUBJECT: Re: The Last Donut
TIME: 12:19 p.m.

Derrick,

I tried to stop by your office, but you weren't there. I've got a hunch on this donut case, so I'll be there to celebrate with yours. Don't eat them all, please.

Thanks,
Jake

FROM: Mindy Delvecchio (m.delvecchio@mildmanneredco.com)
TO: Jake Owens (j.owens@mildmanneredco.com)
SUBJECT: Re: The Last Donut
TIME: 1:45 p.m.

Hi Jake,

Haven't heard from you in a while, so wanted to check in. The client over at Mudspray was so impressed from our call this morning, not only does he want me to lead things on *his* account, he brought on three other accounts for me to handle, too. One of them is run by a "30 under 30" woman—she's famous for inventing the doffle. You know, the donut waffle? I thought that was pretty cool!

Anyway, can you help me get them all set up? I'll need the email aliases going, some background docs . . . all the usual stuff. Give me a shout with any questions.

Thanks,
Mindy

FROM: Jake Owens (j.owens@mildmanneredco.com)
TO: All 12th Floor (all@mildmanneredco.com)
SUBJECT: Re: The Last Donut [.pdf]
TIME: 1:54 p.m.

Hi all,

Attached is a parable about a man who took what was not his. It's quite the riveting read, so I won't spoil it, but I do want to point out that the man receives his comeuppance in the end. Just figured it was apropos of our earlier conversation from this morning. Thanks for reading, and if you'd like to share your thoughts with me, you're more than welcome to.

Jake

FROM: Cassidy Alvarez (c.alvarez@mildmanneredco.com)
TO: Mariah Lane (m.lane@mildmanneredco.com)
SUBJECT: Re: The Last Donut
TIME: 2:02 p.m.

Did you see Jake's email? He's gone completely insane!!

FROM: Mariah Lane (m.lane@mildmanneredco.com)
TO: Cassidy Alvarez (c.alvarez@mildmanneredco.com)
SUBJECT: Re: The Last Donut
TIME: 2:05 p.m.

Yeah, he's losing it, fast. What does a box of donuts cost, like fifteen bucks? This can't be worth all the trouble he's going through.

FROM: Derrick Porter (d.porter@mildmanneredco.com)
TO: Jake Owens (j.owens@mildmanneredco.com)
SUBJECT: Re: The Last Donut
TIME: 3:34 p.m.

Hey buddy,

How are you? I noticed you've been sending emails but haven't stopped back by my office yet. I'll be here for another half hour. If you don't swing by before then, we'll set something up for later in the week. Let's solve what's been bugging you, okay?

All my best,
Derrick

FROM: Grant Atkins (g.atkins@mildmanneredco.com)
TO: All 12th Floor (all@mildmanneredco.com)
SUBJECT: Re: The Last Donut
TIME: 5:54 p.m.

Hi Jake,

Sorry that I'm just seeing this now, but I accidentally knocked those donuts onto the floor this morning. I was pouring a cup of coffee on the table and it started overflowing. So, I reached for the mug to take a quick sip and clean it up a bit, but I accidentally bumped the box of donuts and they tipped over onto the floor. You know how one thing happens and it just sort of snowballs from there? That's my bad.

It's the weirdest thing, though. I gathered them back up and left them on the counter while I ran to the bathroom to get some paper towels for the spilled coffee. Was only gone a minute, maybe two. But when I came back, the donut box was completely empty. So, yes, somebody ate the donuts, but maybe you can take some solace in knowing they were on the floor before they got eaten. And I don't know if you've paid close attention to the break room floor, but it's pretty disgusting. They just kinda toss some Bona floor cleaner on there and call it a day.

Anyway, sorry again for hitting the box on the floor. I'll try to be less clumsy next time. Those coffee mugs sure can be slippery.

Cheers,
Grant

FROM: Mariah Lane (m.lane@mildmanneredco.com)
TO: Cassidy Alvarez (c.alvarez@mildmanneredco.com)
SUBJECT: Re: The Last Donut
TIME: 5:58 p.m.

Blech! I knew those donuts tasted gross. I'm never eating from the break room again.

Off the Bridge

WHEN LUKE PATTON WAS GETTING READY FOR BED ON THE NIGHT of October 16, he didn't do anything out of the ordinary. He brushed his teeth, putting the toothpaste on first before letting the water run on the toothbrush for precisely two seconds. He went to the bathroom because the worst thing one can do before going to bed is to ignore a full bladder. He looked in the mirror and ran his hand over his face, which had a small trace of black stubble. He scratched his head. He read a little bit of the newspaper from that morning. He liked to solve the Jumble; the answer for that day's paper was "ESCARGOT." Pleased with himself, Luke set the paper down on his bedside table. He reached over to the light and clicked it off. He lay his head on the pillow. It was just like any other night.

Except tomorrow, Luke Patton was going to kill himself.

He had been thinking about it for a while now, and the time just seemed right. A few weeks ago, he penned a note detailing his mindset. He wanted people to know they shouldn't blame themselves. There wasn't anything they could do. And he wasn't necessarily depressed, even. He simply found that relationships were extraordinarily hard to maintain, and he hadn't been enjoying conversations he had with people he knew. They all seemed so vapid, so thoroughly unentertaining. If this was the best life would get, why should he stick around? Might as well save himself some time.

Part of the reason Luke had delayed so long in his mission was that he was deciding exactly how he was going to do the deed. He had considered a handgun or a homemade noose in his laundry room. There was a pipe on the ceiling that was perfect for tossing a rope around. He could simply step onto a chair and kick himself free. In fact, he had even tested it out, throwing an extension cord over the pipe and spinning it into a loop. But when he attempted to put his head through the loop, it wouldn't fit. That simply wouldn't do. Luke knew he had to find a different way.

Then, a few weeks ago, he was walking along Thirty-Eighth Street when he saw the bridge. He hadn't thought much of it at the time, other than it meant he should turn around on his walk. It was a walk Luke had taken a hundred times before. He left his place on Twenty-Ninth Street, passing several houses before getting to that final block. He walked past the West Side Liquor Shop, strolled along the side of the Barber Emporium, and crossed the street at Earl's Sandwich and Saxophone Soiree on the corner.

In the past, when he reached the bridge, he turned around and headed back home. This time, he kept going. The bridge was probably about three hundred feet long and led into Laugesville, the neighboring town. More importantly, though, the bridge was roughly sixty feet high. Luke peered over the guard railing. Without even having to get up on his tiptoes, he could see over the edge. There was a small river below, bordered by some grass on either side. The grass was mostly dead; the green had turned an ugly shade of brown. It would only take a little hop up onto the top railing, and then one weightless step until Luke could join that grass.

Luke didn't jump then, though. He had to get some of his affairs in order. He decided October 17 would be the day. It would still be early enough that he could beat the Halloween crowd, but he wanted to collect one last paycheck. That would make his final purchases much easier.

On the morning of his last day on Earth, and wanting to make the most of it, Luke leaped out of bed at 5:24 a.m. and quickly ran to a nearby ATM. It always amazed him how many ATMs were in his city. Every block had at least one, and some had multiple. Everyone wanted money at their fingertips at all times, he guessed.

Luke typed in his password and withdrew all the money he had in his savings account: $1,472. He jogged across the street to Doris's Donuts. A little bell sounded when he opened the door, and the twelve patrons inside, along with Doris herself, looked up. Luke had only been in there once before to order a bear claw. This time he wanted to impress the clientele.

"Hi, Doris," he said, smiling broadly. "I'd like one dozen assorted donuts, please. And I'd also like to buy another dozen for every person in this fine establishment."

Doris ignored Luke and looked back at the customer in line she had been helping. "So, you wanted one cream-filled donut? Sounds good."

Luke stepped toward the register. "Didn't you hear me? I want to buy donuts for everyone in here. A dozen each, please."

Doris raised an eyebrow. "Look," she said, "you might think this is a very noble thing you're doing, but a dozen boxes of donuts is gonna add up for you real quick. It'll be like one hundred and sixty dollars after tax. Most folks that come in here spend a couple of bucks at most. So, you'll understand my hesitation when someone comes in here offering to spend eighty times that."

Luke pulled out his wad of cash. "I get what you're saying—but paying is no trouble. Please, I just want to brighten everyone's day."

"All right, sir," Doris said, "twelve boxes of a dozen donuts each. Assorted, you said?"

"Yes," Luke said. The smile had returned to his face. "That'd be perfect."

"Great," Doris said. "It'll be about an hour wait while we make some more. We only have a handful of donuts left at the moment."

"Oh," Luke said, slightly discouraged. "No matter. I don't mind waiting. And I'm sure the lure of fresh donuts will be enough for all of these good people to stick around."

An hour later, Luke had his dozen boxes of a dozen donuts. Only three patrons from an hour before were still in the store, and nobody else had walked in. They gladly took two boxes each, though one of them required some extra convincing. Luke understood. It's not every day you have a man offering you a batch of free donuts. It made sense that people might be suspicious.

Luke left the store with six boxes in tow, barely able to see above the top of the large stack. He planned to give the rest away to some homeless people he always saw on the block. He went over to the area they normally hung out in, but there was nobody there. *That's strange*, Luke thought. *Maybe they're all somewhere else today.*

Just as he was about to walk away, he saw one man hanging out inside a doorway. Here was the lucky recipient!

"Hello there, sir," Luke said as he approached. "How are you doing today?"

"Oh, can't complain," the man said. "I've got some warmth, it's a beautiful day out, and look at this! A man just came by and gave me this tasty donut. Life is good, my friend."

Luke's face dropped. Someone had beaten him to the punch. No matter. He figured offering a whole box of donuts would surely beat offering one.

"How about an entire box of donuts, then?" Luke said. He opened up the top one to show the man the variety contained inside. "Doesn't that look delicious?"

"Sure," the man said, peering into the box. He held up the half-eaten donut in his hand. "But I've already got one, so I'm good for now."

Luke didn't understand. How could this man not want more than one donut? "Tell you what," Luke said. "You're friends with the people who hang around here, right? Would you mind doing me a favor?"

"That depends." The man eyed Luke cautiously. "What kind of favor are we talking about here?"

Luke's smile returned. "Oh, it's nothing too crazy. I just bought too many donuts—as you can tell—and I was hoping to pass them out to some people who might be hungry and could enjoy them. I only need the one box, and I'm giving away the rest. Since you're all set on donuts, would you be willing to watch these boxes until everyone comes back? Then they can take as many as they want."

The man thought about it for a moment. He rubbed his chin, but Luke couldn't tell if he was thinking or if he was just trying to nab some chocolate icing that had fallen from his lips. "I suppose I could," he said. "But you'd have to make it worth my while. And I was planning on traveling to the other side of town. Can't just be sitting all day."

"I can give you twenty dollars in addition to the boxes," Luke said. "That seems like a pretty fair deal."

He opened up his wallet to take out a twenty, when the man stopped him. "Looks like you've got a little more than that in there," the man said. "Why not make it sixty?"

Luke had already spent more time at the donut shop and having this conversation than he had hoped for. "Fine," he said, pulling out two additional bills. "Sixty dollars. And you'll make sure everyone gets their fill?"

"Sure, sure," the man said. "Everyone will get some." He grabbed the money and ambled away down the block. That wasn't exactly how Luke pictured this whole exchange going. No matter. He had done a good deed, and he was proud of himself. Now, onto the next task.

Luke wanted to look dapper when he was found below the bridge. He had never dressed up—really "dressed to the nines" as his mother liked to say—in his entire life. But first, he needed to freshen up, and that included a haircut and shave at the barbershop.

He passed by one at Thirty-Fourth and Haribow Street, and he liked it because of the big barber pole on the outside. It was always spinning, even when the shop was closed. And more often than not, you could find a friendly guy sitting out front on the steps. Today was no different. Luke offered the man on the steps a donut from his box. He still had ten left and couldn't possibly eat all of them.

The man licked his lips and tapped his fingers together, delicately studying the box. "Ooh, I must say, this jelly-filled one looks like the winner!" He snatched up a donut from the corner of the box faster than a diving hawk plucking a fish out of a lake. After a big first bite, jelly gushed out the back of the donut. He stuck his hand out to make sure he wasn't wasting an ounce of that sweet processed sugar.

Luke smiled. "Glad you like it," he said, continuing up the steps. A small bell sounded when he walked through the door. It made him feel welcome.

"What the hell do you want?" a voice called from the back. Luke wasn't sure where it was coming from. He craned his neck to see behind the barbers who were cutting other people's hair in the chairs up front.

What was the proper way to respond to a question like that? "Um . . . I, uh, . . . I'd like a haircut, please," Luke managed to squeak out.

"Yeah, you and everyone else who comes in here." The voice had finally revealed itself as a small, round, balding man. He walked toward the entrance, wiping his hands on his apron. It was stained from . . . well, Luke didn't know what, exactly. But boy, was it stained. "You got options, though. Do you want shampoo? A shave too? Some stupid pompadour? It's all different costs."

"Uh, a . . . a shave and a cut would be great," Luke said, regaining his confidence just a little. "Nothing too complicated on the hair, either. A small touch up would be perfect."

"Great. Real original," the guy said, spinning a chair in Luke's direction. "Let's get started."

"Oh, and I have donuts, too!" Luke blurted out, holding up the box in his hands.

"Perfect!" the barber said, his expression softening a little. "I was just telling Eddie over there how I was craving a donut, wasn't I, Eddie?"

"Eh?" Another barber briefly looked up at Luke's box. "Eh."

"Let me grab a chocolate old-fashioned. That'll be great," the barber said. "Now, take a seat."

Luke walked over to the chair. He noticed some of the stuffing poking out around the edges. Upon sitting down, he felt lumps all over the seat. At least he wouldn't fall asleep during his haircut. That had happened a couple of times.

The barber had incredibly calloused hands, which Luke figured was due to working with scissors and wooden hairbrushes all the time. As he munched on the donut, the barber was quite liberal with his squirt bottle, spraying water all over Luke's hair. The water started dripping down his neck and face. Luke hated swimming for this exact reason.

The barber used a comb to smooth out Luke's hair, jerking his neck around like an old rag doll. He was deft with his scissors, trimming stray hairs with surprising speed. He barely spoke, but Luke heard occasional mutters, including "another knot?" and "using too much conditioner." Luke didn't have a response for that one. He used conditioner every time he showered.

While he was debating whether or not he should apologize for his uncooperative hair, another man walked into the barbershop. The man working on Luke's hair stopped and walked over to the new guest, leaving one side of hair uneven and a comb sticking straight up from the center of Luke's head. Luke silently counted his blessings, thankful the barber had left the comb in his hair, not the scissors.

"Ernie, you sonofabitch!" the barber said, greeting the man with a great big bear hug. "How the hell are ya? It's been ages!"

"Oh, about the same old, same old, you old bastard," Ernie said. "Wanted to see if I could come get a haircut if it wasn't too much trouble for your old crotchety self."

"Of course not," the barber replied, walking back to Luke. "Let me just finish up with this guy, and I'll get started with you. He brought donuts. They're over there on the counter."

"Oh, that wasn't for other customers…" Luke said.

The barber glared at him. "Now you listen to me. Ernie, he's a good guy. I've known him for forty years. You, I've known for forty seconds. For all I know you'll never come in here again. You'll probably skip town or jump off a bridge or something. He's earned a donut."

Once again, Luke found himself without a valid response. Even if he weren't planning to jump off a bridge tonight, he certainly wouldn't come back to this barbershop.

He looked over at Ernie, who had situated himself in another barber chair. He had procured a newspaper and was paging through it as he bit on an éclair. His weathered hands and wrinkly face suggested a well-lived life. He looked up and caught Luke staring at him.

He put down the paper and studied Luke. "You aren't too bright, are you, kid? Here's a tip: Don't move while you're getting shaved. You look like the kind of guy who's never actually used a razor in his life. Now you've got a few whiskers and want to get rid of 'em. That's fine, but one wrong move, and yecchh!" As he said this, he drew his finger across his neck in a slashing motion.

Luke perked up in his chair. He thought for a moment that perhaps causing his barber to slash his throat could be a good way to go, as the barber would have both literal and figurative blood on his hands. But no, that sounded more painful than simply jumping off a bridge. Plus, it would be really awkward while waiting to bleed out. Would he have to make small talk?

The shave did feel nice, though. A warm lather engulfed his face, and again, the barber was very slick with his hands. It almost felt like a massage, rather than hairs being scraped off his chin. Luke was still on edge about what Ernie had said to him, though, and kept his posture rigid. He worried leaning back would certainly do him in.

"All right, we're done," the barber said, whisking away the smock that had been covering Luke's body. "Cut and a shave, and you know what? You're not looking half bad. Can you believe it, Ernie?"

"He's got a pro behind the scissors!" Ernie said from across the room. "You can make anybody look good, even a doughface like this kid."

Luke ran a hand over his cheek. He pretended like he was testing the thoroughness of the shave, but he was just trying to figure out what a "doughface" was. He thought he had a rather well-defined jawline. Maybe he had been wrong all along.

"When you're done admiring my work, I'll be at the till," the barber said. "Fifty bucks for the cut and shave."

"Fifty dollars?" Luke was doing some quick math in his head. He'd still have a good amount of money for his other purchases, but again, this was more than he had planned to spend.

"Yeah, and that ain't including tip," the barber said. Luke reached into his pocket and pulled out three twenty-dollar bills. He wasn't sure why he was tipping, exactly, but he told the barber to keep the change. "Hey, look at that! Sonofabitch gave me ten dollars as a tip.

That's nearly enough to get me a new pair of dull scissors. Tell you what, though, that was a pretty tasty donut. You're not the worst I've seen, kid!"

Luke hardly considered that a compliment, but he didn't want to stick around and press his luck. He grabbed the box of donuts and headed toward his next stop: the tailor. He had never owned a suit and wanted to look good for whoever found him. The tailor was only a couple of blocks down the road, along the way toward his final destination. Luke took a deep breath before stepping inside. Immediately he was greeted with gentle classical music over the speakers and by a thin man with an even thinner mustache.

"Hello, good sir!" the man bellowed. "What can I do for you on this fine evening?"

Luke thought that was an odd thing to say, considering it was about 2:30 in the afternoon. But he did appreciate the enthusiasm and, most of all, the kindness. That was a trait lacking in most other people he had come across.

"My good man," Luke said, echoing the greeter's tone, "I'd like to purchase a suit for myself to wear out on the town during this wonderful evening." The man frowned slightly. Did he think Luke was mocking him?

"Very well then, sir," the tailor said, in a much more somber tone. "Let's take a look at what we have, shall we?"

Luke was confused by this sudden change in the man's behavior, but he followed him to a rack of suits. "Now, have you ever bought a suit before?" the man said. Luke guessed he already knew the answer.

"No," Luke said sheepishly. "In fact, I've never even worn a suit before, if you can believe that!"

The man nodded, confirming that, yes, he could in fact believe that. "Very well then, sir." He left the rack they were looking at and hightailed it to the back of the store. Looking back over his shoulder, he called out to Luke, "Follow me, please."

He brought Luke to a woman who was standing in the back of the store. She had one pencil over an ear and another one in her mouth. Upon seeing Luke approaching, she extended a hand. "I'm Cheryl. Pleased to meet you," she said.

"Hi Cheryl. I'm Luke." He realized he came across as too eager, but he was doing his best not to mimic how Cheryl had introduced herself. He didn't want to offend yet another person today. "I'm here to get a suit, but I have no idea where to even start."

"That's no problem," Cheryl said. "We'll start by taking your measurements. That way you'll know what will fit you. And trust me, you want a suit that fits."

Cheryl retrieved a tape measure and began working it around Luke, checking his arms, shoulders, torso, waist, inseam, and a few other measurements he didn't quite understand, but figured they were necessary for the perfect suit. He did his best to not giggle while Cheryl was taking his measurements. The tape measure tickled more than he thought it would, but he didn't want to come across as rude by laughing.

"You sure are squirmy," Cheryl said, snapping the tape measure back into its holder. "But we're done here. Forty-two chest, thirty-six waist, and forty-two hips. I'm writing it down on this piece of paper, so you won't forget. It'll help you with your search. Best of luck!"

Luke took the slip of paper back to the man who had greeted him initially. "I've learned a little more about myself!" Luke said, chuckling at his statement. The man gave him a blank look as he took the paper from his hands.

"Very well, sir," he said. "I think you'll look best in a standard dark gray suit. A man of your stature can be a little creative with his suits, but with your complexion, dark gray or maybe charcoal is the way to go. Here, try this jacket on."

Luke put on the jacket and immediately felt a change surge

through him. So, this is what royalty felt like. The jacket seemed like it was made for him.

"Wow, I'm actually speechless," the man said. "No extra room in the shoulders, and the arms are the exact right length. This is a terrific fit. How does it feel on you?"

"Like a million bucks!" Luke said, giving a thumbs up. "Do suits always fit this well on the first try?"

"Not at all," the man said. "Usually they're only so-so, and we have to do adjustments here and there. A little lengthening of the sleeves, widening of the shoulders, and so on. But too much and it can ruin a suit. When you find one that fits you, you should cherish it for the rest of your life."

Luke thought that wouldn't be a lot of time to cherish his suit, but he was excited to be on the path toward looking great. "Don't I need some pants, too?"

The man looked at Luke the way a child looks at a parent that's being particularly embarrassing. "Obviously. Unless you're only planning to interact with people from the waist up. You'll also need a shirt and tie and, likely, dress socks and shoes, too. Please don't take this the wrong way, but it looks like you've never dressed up nicely at any point in your life. Am I wrong?"

Luke sadly shook his head. "No, that's why it's so important to find a nice suit. I don't have socks or shoes, either."

"That's easy enough to take care of," the man said, pulling out a Brannock Device. He had Luke put his feet in, one at a time. "Oh dear, it looks like your left is just over eleven, and your right is a twelve. Let's get you a pair of size twelves in black. Might add a bit of room in the left one but I'd rather have that than you walking around in pain all the time."

"Thank you, sir," Luke said. The man was talking about the shoes, but his words seemed particularly poignant.

"In the meantime, go ahead and try these on," the man said, picking up a dress shirt and a pair of pants off the rack and handing them to Luke. "I'll go get you some socks and shoes and a nice belt, too. But make sure these fit first."

Much like the suit jacket, the pants fit Luke perfectly, though he found the sleeves on the dress shirt to be a little long. When he walked outside the changing area to model them in the mirror, Cheryl came up behind him.

"Looking good!" she said. "We found you some shoes and socks, a belt, and a tie. With how well these are fitting, you'll be able to get out of here wearing your suit! Normally we have to hold onto it for a few days to make alterations."

Luke hadn't considered that. He would have hated for his suit to change his schedule for tonight. "Thanks! I'd like to wear it out. It really is comfortable, and I like how it looks quite a bit."

"Likewise. Very snazzy," Cheryl said. Luke thought she was merely being professional but appreciated the compliment. "We'll want to shorten those sleeves just a little bit, though. If they're too long they can bunch up and make you look sloppy. I'm happy to make those alterations now, if you don't mind waiting around a bit."

"Oh no, I don't mind," Luke said. "I don't have anywhere to be until tonight."

"Perfect!" Cheryl said. "This shouldn't take very long at all."

While Cheryl was fixing his shirt, Luke moseyed around the shop. He picked up some other jackets to try them on, just out of curiosity. All of them were either baggy or too tight, so he really appreciated finding a good one.

After taking off a particularly loose suit jacket, Luke headed to the tie rack. The shop had several ties on a spinning motor. Luke admired the variety in front of him. A row of dark, solid colors stood in stark contrast to a variety of floral and pastel designs. Luke always thought he'd wind up wearing ties with fun designs on them, like ones featuring a cartoon character, but he liked the more dignified look of the basic ones. Still, he didn't trust himself to pick out the right one so would be happy with whatever Cheryl pulled for him.

After close to an hour, Cheryl came back out with the shirt.

"Okay, this should be good to go!" she said. "Try it with the tie and shoes, too. Let's see the full look."

Moments later, Luke was beaming into the mirror. "I love it!" Luke said. "Thanks so much for all of your help."

"My pleasure," the woman said, smiling in a more subdued manner. "Let's get you checked out . . . jacket . . . dress shirt . . . pants . . . shoes . . . socks . . . belt . . . tie . . . tie clip . . . and a pocket square for good measure. All of that comes to . . . one thousand and eighty-nine dollars."

Luke's eyes widened. "Wow, I didn't realize a suit was so expensive," he said, chuckling nervously.

"Do you . . . do you not have the money for it?" the woman asked, raising an eyebrow. "We do take credit cards, you know. This isn't the 1930s."

"Oh, I've actually got cash!" Luke said, pulling the wad from his pocket. He spent a solid four minutes counting out $1,089. The biggest bills were only twenty dollars, so it was quite a bit of math to do. The woman stared at the pile, then switched her glance to Luke. Her perplexed look remained.

"Very well," she said. "I've actually never seen someone pay in cash for a full suit. Guess there's a first time for everything."

"Thanks!" Luke said, smiling. "I'm excited to wear my brand-new suit!"

"Just watch out for the weather," the woman said as Luke headed toward the exit. "I hear it might rain tonight."

That made Luke upset. He didn't want his suit to get too soiled. Hopefully the rain would hold off for another day or two.

His final order of business before heading to the bridge was to order a nice steak dinner. Some of Luke's finest childhood memories were of his dad cooking steaks on the grill during the summer. His dad taught him that a well-done steak was only for fools, but Luke couldn't stand to eat anything else. He always ordered his steaks well-done, and for his final meal, he was going to try one cooked medium. He wanted to make his dad proud.

About a block away from the bridge, Isabel's had just opened up. Their crown jewel was the filet mignon, which you could coat with crab. Luke thought that was a bit much; the steak by itself would be enough.

"Hello, sir. Table for one?" said a tall, lanky man with a wispy mustache. Luke nodded. "Right this way, sir." Luke followed the man to a small table for two. He figured it wasn't very practical to just have solo tables, but the extra chair stared back at him, mocking his loneliness.

"Your server will be right with you, sir," the man said, placing a menu in Luke's hands. "Please, enjoy your meal."

Luke's server soon sauntered over to the table. She looked like she had just yelled at someone and was proud of it. "Hello, sir," she said, feigning a smile. "What can I get you?"

"I've got . . . one hundred and three dollars left," Luke said, taking out the remaining handful of bills in his pocket. "What'll that get me?"

"A filet mignon, a Coke, and enough to tip me nearly one hundred percent," the server said. "How does that sound?"

"Make it a tequila sunrise instead of a Coke," Luke said. He had never tried a tequila sunrise before, but always thought the name sounded refreshing. "I'm celebrating tonight."

"Perfect," the server said. Luke was glad she didn't ask what he was celebrating. "How would you like your steak prepared?"

"Well d— medium, please." He handed back the menu and gave a firm nod, as if he did this all the time.

"Very well, sir," his server said. "I'll have your drink right out to you and get the rest of your order in."

A few minutes later, his drink arrived. Luke picked up the straw that was delivered alongside it and tried to tear at the wrapping. He couldn't quite get his fingernails to rip it, and after much gnawing at the edges, he finally undid the protective sheath. He put the straw into his drink, but no liquid was coming out, no matter how hard he pursed his lips around the opening. He took the straw back out of the drink and realized the bottom of his straw hadn't been cut correctly. It was sealed, making it effectively useless. These were the little, stupid things that kept irritating him.

He picked up the glass and took a big swig from his drink, sans straw. He was impressed—tequila sunrises were pretty tasty!

His server came back with his meal. She plopped it down in front of him. "Can I get you anything else?" she said, already in the process of moving away from the table.

"Um, some steak sauce would be great," Luke said. "Just a little bit."

"We have bottles, so you can have however little bit you want."

She scurried off and returned with a bottle of steak sauce that was nearly empty. Luke didn't even have a chance to lift it up before she disappeared again. He pounded the bottom of the bottle and a scant amount of sauce came out onto his plate. This would have to do.

Luke attacked his steak. Even with the steak knife, it was pretty tough to cut through, and the inside looked closer to black than pink. "Huh," he said aloud. "I wonder if they made a mistake."

Luke looked around for the server but couldn't find her. Not wanting his meat to get cold, he choked down his first bite, having to chew it for nearly a minute before he could swallow. The following bites were even tougher for him to cut, but Luke kept at it. He wanted to experience this steak in full, even if it meant sawing at it like a lumberjack going at a piece of wood.

His steak sauce ran out by the third bite, and the only time his server came by was to take back the bottle of steak sauce. She didn't even check on how he was enjoying things.

As Luke shoveled the final piece of steak into his mouth, the server walked up to the table. "You know, this is a little embarrassing," she said, "but I accidentally dropped off the wrong steak to your table. That one was for another guy who wanted his really well done, like totally blackened. Looks like you enjoyed yours, though!" She pointed at his now-empty plate. *That certainly explains a lot,* Luke thought. He looked up at her. "Yeah, I guess . . ."

"Great! Can I get you anything else?" his server asked. "I hope not, since that'll be coming out of my tip." She gave him a playful nudge and dropped the bill on the table.

"No, I'm done, I suppose," he said, mustering a smile. She didn't deserve a good tip, but he wasn't going to use the money, so he figured he'd do a nice thing and give her all he had left. Plus, he really enjoyed the tequila sunrise. He took the wad of bills out of his pocket. "Here you go. Don't spend it all in one place!"

The server took the cash and rifled through it. She dropped three twenty-dollar bills into her pocket and slipped the rest into the bill. Luke looked up at her, confused. "Don't worry about it," the server said, waving a hand at him. "Have a good evening!"

Luke thanked her and got up from his seat. Despite the effort it took to consume his entire steak, he did feel full. He deemed it a satisfactory final meal. Luke left the restaurant and headed toward the bridge on Thirty-Eighth Street. He walked past the West Side Liquor Shop, strolled along the side of the Barber Emporium, and crossed the street at Earl's Sandwich and Saxophone Soiree on the corner.

He saw the faint gleam of the bridge in the darkness of the night. It was probably close to seven o'clock by now, and the lights of the city flickered in the distance. Some sound reached him, but the bridge was oddly quiet, save for a few cars occasionally passing by.

Luke looked upward into the nighttime sky. It was a beautiful, clear night, with stars beaming brightly overhead. Luke traced between a few with his fingers, not drawing anything in particular. He relished these last moments of physical connection with the cosmos.

He ran his hand along the guardrail. It was wet from the evening's mist, and Luke wiped the moisture onto his pant leg. He peered over the edge. He couldn't really make out the grass below, but he knew it was there. It would serve as a nice landing spot.

Luke took a step up. The guardrail had three rungs on it, and he was now standing on the bottom one. He wondered if it would hurt when he fell. Surely this bridge was tall enough that he'd expire upon impact, right?

Luke moved his feet up onto the second rung of the guardrail. He was beginning to shake a little bit now, but he wasn't sure if it was from nerves or from being on an unsteady platform. He thought about after he jumped. Who would find him? He hoped it wasn't a child. That would be a traumatic thing to see so young. If a child were to stumble upon him, maybe he'd think Luke was sleeping. *It will all depend on how I land*, he thought. He made a mental note to try and sprawl himself wide to make it seem as if he were sleeping.

Luke took the last step he could without actually stepping off the bridge. He was now on the third rung. His suit jacket was flapping in the wind. It wasn't a strong breeze, but enough to let you know it was there. Luke looked down. Sixty feet up in the air and not a single car around to witness what he was about to do. It was exactly how he hoped it would be.

Okay, he thought. *This is it. You're here. Time to do this.*

He crouched down, a mix between a gargoyle and a tiger waiting to pounce. After a long pause, he sprung off the guardrail.

For a moment, he felt as nearly high up as the stars. He stopped hearing any sound around him, including his own thoughts. He was completely free.

Luke landed with a thud, face down on the ground. Unable to

see, he felt around with his hands. They didn't touch grass, or even dirt. His hands were feeling asphalt. Luke slowly lifted his head from the pavement. A man was standing a few feet away with a bewildered look on his face.

"Are you crazy?!" the man shouted. "What do you think you're doing? Are you trying to fly? Are you drunk? You could have been killed!"

Luke rubbed his forehead. "Wait . . . did I jump? Where am I?" He was still a little shell-shocked. Did he land on a road down below?

"You tried to!" the man replied, still shouting. His roaring voice echoed through the still of the night. "Luckily I was driving by and saw you standing up there. If you weren't wearing that nice suit, I probably wouldn't have been able to get ahold of you. But I grabbed your jacket and yanked you over the railing and back onto the street here. You really could have hurt yourself!"

Luke was flattered that he got a compliment on his suit. "Well . . . thanks, I guess."

"Hey, wait a minute," the man said. "You're that guy from Doris's Donuts! You came in and bought a bunch of donuts for everyone there. I knew you looked familiar."

"Yep, that's me," Luke said. "How'd you like the donuts?"

"They were great! I gave a few away to some friends I met up with later, but I made sure to save one for tonight. It's their triple-chocolate glazed one. It's my favorite."

"That's great," Luke said. He sighed, his shoulders heaving. He still hadn't gotten up yet; he was sitting on the street, toying with his pant leg.

"What's the matter, man?" his rescuer said. "You seem upset."

"If I can be totally honest with you," Luke said. "I wasn't trying to fly while I was up on that guardrail. I'm not drunk, and I'm not on drugs or anything. I wanted to kill myself. I was tired of living, that's all."

The man took a step back. "Damn, man . . . I didn't know. I thought for sure you were falling or something. I saved you, and really all you wanted was someone to let you go."

Luke thought that had a nice poetic beauty to it. "Something like that, yeah. It's not your fault. You didn't know. It's just . . . "

"Yeah, what is it?" the man said. "We're friends now. You can tell me."

"I spent all my money today," Luke said. "I took out my entire savings to do special things, like get this suit and buy everyone donuts. I literally have nothing left. Which would be fine if I were dead, but now I'm alive. And . . . I'm actually glad. When I jumped, there was some regret. You've given me a second chance, but it's going to be rough. I don't have any money. I quit my job. I don't even really have any friends."

"Oh, man, that's a bummer," the man said, shaking his head. Suddenly, his eyes lit up. "I'll tell you what you *do* have, though!" He went to his car. Luke rolled himself out of the street and leaned up against the guardrail. The man grabbed something from the front seat. "Look!" he said. "It's the triple-chocolate glazed donut I was saving. Let's split it!"

Luke smiled. A donut did sound delicious right now. And this man was demonstrating there were some good people in the world. Maybe Luke hadn't been looking for them hard enough. Maybe things would turn out all right after all. "I'd love that!" Luke said, beaming.

"Perfect. Here you go," the man said, offering Luke half of the donut. Luke took a bite and the rest of the donut broke off. It fell to the ground, a small *pffft* ensuing as it broke into pieces on the road.

"Oh man, that's a bummer," the man said, looking at the remnants of the donut. "But hey, at least you got to enjoy one bite. Take care of yourself, man, okay?" He patted Luke on the shoulder and walked back to his car. Luke watched as he drove away.

Luke looked at the donut one more time. He shook his head and headed back down the street, trudging slowly toward his apartment.

When he got back home, he brushed his teeth, putting the toothpaste on first before letting the water run on it for precisely two seconds. He went to the bathroom because the worst thing one can do before going to bed is to ignore a full bladder. He looked in the mirror and ran his hand over his face, which had a small trace of black stubble. He scratched his head. He read a little bit of the newspaper from that morning. The Jumble answer for that day's paper was "PARSNIPS." Luke set the paper down on his bedside table. He reached over to the bedside lamp and clicked it off.

But tonight was different. Luke loved the way his suit felt on him and wanted to sleep in it. He laid on his back, staring up at the ceiling. His hands were folded over his waist, his fingers interlocking as they rested on his stomach. Luke's mind had been racing all day. Now, he was peaceful. He could only think of how calm everything felt in this one serene moment.

Luke let out a deep breath and closed his eyes.

Pop Quiz

"ALL RIGHT, CLASS. THAT WAS THE BELL. I'LL SEE YOU TOMORROW. And remember! We have a pop quiz on Monday. Do the homework questions from chapter six over the weekend. They'll be a big help. Don't forget, my office is always open if you need me, assuming you need me during office hours, which, I'll say it again, are from three to four in the afternoon. Sally, I know you want to come at 2:30, but I simply will not be there. Thanks for understanding. Let's go, people! Get a move on!"

Mr. Patterstone clapped his hands, hoping the sound would cause his students to vacate his classroom more quickly. He really did enjoy teaching algebra, but sometimes it seemed like he was talking to a brick wall. This particular class had very few students who gave any real effort, and the ones who did, like Sally Moffins, were irritating beyond belief.

Mr. Patterstone said goodbye to the last student leaving the room, a particularly slow dolt named Eddie Montgomery. He was a good kid, and his heart was in the right place, but algebra just wasn't for him. Mr. Patterstone thought he'd make a great career out of being a test subject—the result of sustaining too many concussions on the football field.

Once Eddie left, Mr. Patterstone slumped into the seat at his desk. It was an old, beaten-up office chair, and it creaked every time he sat down, moved around, or breathed. He had gotten so used to the squeaking sound he almost considered it his classes' signature soundtrack. He flipped open his laptop and powered it on.

"MAN, MR. PATTERSTONE is such a jerk," Louis Finnegan said out in the hall. "What's he doing giving us a test on a Monday? That means the whole weekend is shot to study."

"It's what mean teachers do," Cindy Hubbard said. "They love seeing that look of frustration. Why else do you think algebra is so hard? We don't actually need it. It exists just so teachers like Mr. Patterstone can laugh at us and give dumb pop quizzes."

"I do like that he sees through Sally's brown-nosing, though," Mike Owens said. He was one of six kids named Mike in the class, though he stood out by being the tallest. "She's always putting on that goody-two-shoes act, and teachers keep falling for it. At least he keeps her from doing that."

"Yeah, but I still don't like having him as my teacher," Tiffany Rodriguez said, popping a piece of gum into her mouth and blowing a bubble. "He's just so . . . *boring!*"

"PLEASE TELL ME YOU'RE READY to go. This shouldn't be taking so long."

"Will you just relax? There's nobody here but us. Just calm down and keep a lookout, okay?" Mr. Patterstone shook his head. Chris always got a little jumpy when they were on a mission. But they had robbed twenty-two jewelry stores so far, without getting caught. Clearly, they knew what they were doing.

Dalton's head poked out from behind a rear door. "Whoa, did

you know there was a back room in here, too?" He was the newest member of the crew, and, like any other person eager to make friends, he bugged everyone else. But he was highly adept at getting into safes and other secure spots, so the team was glad to have him. "Must be another four hundred pieces of jewelry just hanging out in here."

"If there's anything good in there, take one piece—two, tops!" Mr. Patterstone whispered. "We don't have enough time to be fooling around here."

The team had been committing robberies for about a year and a half. Dalton joined the group eight months ago—before him, it had been a trio of Mr. Patterstone, Chris, and Glider. "Glider" wasn't his actual name, of course, but nobody really knew what was on his birth certificate. He was the real brains behind the operation, scoping out targets, mapping routes, and performing the tiniest incisions into glass display cases to sneak out only a few small prizes.

That was something Mr. Patterstone had come to admire. As a high school teacher, he wasn't exactly raking in the big bucks. It was tempting to go for the gusto on the initial robbery, but Glider was insistent on keeping the amount taken to a minimum.

"Think about it," he had said that first night. "This jeweler comes back tomorrow and sees shattered glass everywhere, what's he going to do? Report it immediately. He knows someone's broken in by all the damage. He knows he's been robbed—and knowing is the first step to finding out who's done the crime."

"So, we're only going to take a couple pieces?" Mr. Patterstone said, his head tilted in confusion. "That doesn't make sense!"

"Makes perfect sense," Glider said. "And we're not taking the most valuable stuff, either. Look at some of the things in here. Necklaces made out of solid, twenty-four karat gold. This owner probably comes over to those pieces every single day, just to check that they're still there. And with good reason; they cost like five grand each! What we're taking is good, though. We pick up a few rings, a couple of lockets, a few of the lesser diamonds—we're still looking at about a haul of ten grand. The best part? Because we're being precise and keyed in on the right stuff, this sap will have no idea any of those pieces are even gone."

Mr. Patterstone had worried back then at the thought of having to rob multiple stores in order to get the money he needed. He wanted to finally pay off his home mortgage, which was sitting at about eighty thousand dollars. With his salary, it would have taken another twenty-five years or so. He told himself this was merely accelerating the pace. But two months ago, Mr. Patterstone hit that eighty thousand threshold. Now he was doing these jobs because they gave him a thrill he'd never felt before in his life. There was a rush that came from measuring the exact angle he'd need to successfully wedge a pair of tweezers into a case to nab a silver medallion that a simple algebra problem couldn't provide.

"Would you stop jumping around, Chris?" Mr. Patterstone said. "You're making me nervous. Look, Glider and I are just going to pick up these couple of necklaces here, and then we'll get out, okay? We've gotten a good haul. Just let us know if you see anything."

"Aw, man, I got a bad feeling about this," Chris said. "Something don't seem right."

"You say that every time," Dalton said. "There's nothing different about this job than any other one we've done. It's gonna be fine."

"All of you really need to shut up," Glider said. He was holding a bold, shimmering bracelet. "I'm done with my extractions. By my count, it's about thirty thousand, and we're still leaving a ton intact. You done yet, Patterstone?"

Mr. Patterstone slid the tweezers back into his pocket. He tossed a sapphire to Glider. "Yep. Take a look at that."

"Not bad, Patterstone," Glider said, examining the stone in his gloved hand. "Not bad at all. This is shaping up to be our best job yet." Right as he uttered the final word, the team heard sirens off in the distance.

"Oh, man, I knew it!" Chris yelled. "I'm getting outta here!" He bolted toward the rear exit, nearly knocking over an entire tower of customizable key chains in the process. The door slammed behind him with a thud. The rest of the team hadn't even moved from their positions.

"Just stay calm," Glider said. "We don't move; they won't see us."

The approaching sirens wailed louder. Mr. Patterstone guessed they were only a block away now. He felt the muscles in his throat tighten. Instinctively, even though he knew it wouldn't really help, he pressed himself up against a wall. If he stayed thin, maybe the cops would miss him.

The flash of the lights was blinding. Mr. Patterstone shut his eyes, but he could still see the red and blue flickers, alternating in a sea of color. He forced one eye back open and saw Dalton ducked under the same tower Chris had nearly knocked over. Glider was crouched down behind a display case, reaching for the gun tucked in his waistband. Then, just as quickly as they'd come, the lights disappeared. Mr. Patterstone craned his neck, trying to peek out the window. The police cars turned left down the street and flew out of sight.

"Phew, that was a little closer than usual, huh?" Mr. Patterstone said as the team headed out the door. "Now let's get moving. I've got a pop quiz to write."

"OKAY, CLASS, I HOPE YOU'VE done your studying. This quiz is a bit harder than usual because I really want you to apply yourselves today."

An audible groan rose from the students. Tiffany Rodriguez and Cindy Hubbard shot each other a look. They had gone to the mall in lieu of studying. Louis Finnegan leaned his head back and howled, hoping somebody would hear and come to save him from what lay ahead.

"Calm down, people," Mr. Patterstone said. "It's just a pop quiz. Twelve questions. Nobody's going to jail. If you finish early, bring your test up to me and keep yourselves busy and your eyes forward. No jumping around. I know some of you love to do that, but let's all just relax, okay?"

Mr. Patterstone began handing out the quizzes, providing a stack to the student at the front of each row. "Now take one and pass it behind you." When he arrived at the final row, he started counting out six sheets.

"New watch, Mr. Patterstone?" Mike Owens asked. He was sitting up front in the last row of desks.

Mr. Patterstone pulled back his sleeve, unveiling a shiny, brand new wristwatch. It had been in the backroom loot that Dalton recovered. "Yes, it is, Mike. What do you think?"

"I think you should probably have gone with a smart watch," Mike said. "They can do a lot more than just tell the time. Your phone can even do that. In fact, I think I saw that exact watch at the mall the other day and it cost a ton—like I could have bought a new laptop and had money left over for a couple of video games, too. Why would you waste so much on a regular old watch?"

"I thought this one was pretty nice, and I never had a good watch growing up," Mr. Patterstone said. "Let's consider this a long overdue birthday present."

"If you say so," Mike replied. "But you must have robbed a bank to buy it."

Mr. Patterstone chuckled as he handed the quizzes to Mike. "No, not robbing any banks," he said. "Where do you even get an idea like that?"

"Just a silly thought, I guess," Mike said. "I mean, imagine you robbing a bank or, uh, I don't know, a jewelry store. No offense, sir, but I don't think you could pull it off. You're way more at home here in the classroom. Not that there's anything wrong with that. It's just those high-pressure stakes, they're not for you."

"Don't think I can handle myself, huh?" Mr. Patterstone said. "You wouldn't consider dealing with a classroom full of rowdy kids a stressful situation?"

"I've never had to teach a classroom full of kids, but no. I wouldn't think it's the same thing," Mike said. "If you make a mistake here, you come back the next day and try again. But if you made a mistake robbing a jewelry store, you'd go to jail."

"I suppose it's all a moot point anyway, since I'm not stealing any jewelry," Mr. Patterstone said. "Like you said, I wouldn't be able to handle myself in that situation. Now hurry up and take your quiz. We don't have time to be fooling around here."

Mike took a quiz from the stack of papers and passed the rest to the student behind him. He turned to Sally Moffins, who sat one desk over. "Hey, Sally, don't you think it's a little strange that Mr. Patterstone has that new watch?" he asked. "I've heard what these teachers make—it's not enough to be spending frivolously like that."

"Eyes forward, Mike," Sally said. She was already done with her quiz and was looking straight ahead.

"It just seems a little strange to me, is all," Mike said. "I think there's something going on here."

"The only thing that's going on is *you're* not ready for this quiz, and you're trying to drag me down with you," Sally said. "And I won't be a part of it. Now stop talking!"

Mr. Patterstone listened to this conversation from his desk. He smiled to himself—maybe Sally Moffins wasn't so bad, after all.

Clayton and Sarge

IT WAS A BEAUTIFUL THURSDAY AFTERNOON, UNSEASONABLY warm for the area. Sunlight flooded the neighborhood, which meant kids were allowed to go outside and play. And that meant trouble.

Clayton was an eight-year-old who liked to get into mischief, as most eight-year-old boys do. But Clayton wasn't your typical mischief maker, doing things like drawing on the walls, sneaking a quarter from the teacher's purse, or sticking a Skittle up his nose.

No, Clayton's mischief was far more sinister. Just in the past three months, he had driven his dad's truck to the store to steal jelly beans, he'd cut a large hole in his mom's favorite shirt because "it needed a polka dot," and he had brought a dead bird to school and put it on a classmate's desk.

And every time he got yelled at, he'd reply with the same thing. "I told ya, *I* didn't do anything. It was Sarge!" Sometimes he'd accompany that statement with a dramatic waving of his arms, gesturing wildly at nothing in particular.

The oddest part of it all was that most people believed Clayton. And that was strange because Sarge was the boy's pet dog. He was a black lab, loyal to a fault. Oftentimes, he would just lie at Clayton's feet while the boy was in the plotting stages of his mischief. Then

Sarge would tag along, and Clayton would always pin any blame on his dog. Sarge, being the loyal dog that he was, would take it without so much as a whimper.

Earlier in the week, Clayton had drawn a giant middle finger on the blackboard and signed his artistic masterpiece with "Clayton." Yet he still blamed Sarge for the incident. And with that, his teacher phoned his parents' house, explaining that Sarge was a bad influence on the boy. How could Clayton be expected to learn when he had a mutt impeding his progress?

Clayton's parents took Sarge out to the doghouse and sat him down. They had a stern conversation with him, wagging their fingers extremely close to his nose. Sarge cocked his head to the side and raised an eyebrow, not understanding what he had done. The parents scolded him for nearly half an hour before making him stay in the doghouse all night long.

On that sunny Thursday, Clayton was building anthills in the backyard. He did this by sneaking into neighbors' yards, picking up the ants on their anthills, sticking the ants into a jar, and carrying them back to his house. After having canvassed a couple of blocks, Clayton was overseeing a colony of about twenty-three hundred ants. And Sarge had followed at his heels the whole trek.

Clayton enjoyed watching the ants frantically moving back and forth, their eccentric pace amusing him. When it seemed like they were close to being able to rest, Clayton would knock the tops of the mounds down. A barrage of ants would come scattering out of the hill, working together to rebuild.

Clayton had developed six or seven sizable anthills in the backyard, and he stood surveying the scene. His ultimate goal was to have anthills all over the backyard so no one could step safely in the grass without risking getting ants in their pants. He smiled at his progress so far.

He yelled for his mom to come outside. "Moooooooooommmmmmmmm!" he liked to shout, because he knew she'd come running at the drop of a hat. And when she bolted outside, he was already halfway around the other side of the house. But this was his plan all along. He snuck inside to grab a book of matches from the kitchen counter. He had to stand on his tippy toes to reach them, but he nabbed the book. It had a picture of a star wearing sunglasses on it, which made it seem extra cool to Clayton.

Clayton checked inside the matchbook as he walked back around the house. There were six matches left. He took one out and lit it, striking the match against the book a few times until a flame emerged. Clayton held the match in front of his eyes, watching the fire slowly dissipate.

"Ouch!" Clayton said, as he stumbled over some tools his dad had left in the backyard, sending him tumbling to the earth. His father loved to do yard work, but he was so bad about putting things away. He had kept out his lawn mower and a couple of cans. Clayton wasn't sure what was in them, but he knew he knocked out some liquid onto the grass. Hopefully his dad wouldn't mind.

Upon returning to the anthills, Clayton looked over his assembled creation. Somehow it seemed like there were even more ants now, all scurrying about. Clayton lit a match and turned to Sarge.

"Sarge, ol' boy," he said, "hold onto your hat—we're about to have us some fun. How silly are these ants? Look at them. Running back and forth, never stopping. If I kick some dirt onto them or break up their hill, you'd think they'd leave. But no, they keep sticking around."

Sarge responded by yawning and lying down in the grass near the anthill. He was such a good listener.

"Anyway, Sarge," Clayton said, "I hope you're ready to witness something really cool. I'm gonna hold this match up close to this anthill so I can make these ants dance. I told ya before, you gotta show 'em who's boss. If they don't know, they'll never listen. You really gotta—ouch!"

The flame from the match had risen up to Clayton's fingers, and he dropped it onto the ground near the anthill. "Look what you made me do, Sarge!" he yelled at the dog.

In a flash, a bright orange flame erupted on the lawn. The flame was headed straight toward the anthill. Sarge leapt back, yelping in excitement. He sang to the sky, and each bark was louder than the last.

"My ants!" Clayton yelled. All of his work was about to go up in flames. He clawed at the ground, his fingernails tearing at the dirt as he worked to reroute the flames away from the anthills. Eventually, the flames began turning away toward another part of the lawn.

Clayton stood up and wiped sweat off his forehead. A trace of mud remained as he removed his hand. Sarge continued to bark. Clayton looked back at where Sarge was facing. The flame he had rerouted had now consumed the woodshed, where his family kept tools, toys, and a whole lot of other things they would hate to lose.

"Sarge! What did you do?" Clayton yelled.

Smoke billowed in the air as the shed became further engulfed in flames. Clayton ran to grab the hose from the side of the house and turned the spigot all the way to full power. He sprinted toward the flaming shed, his finger on the trigger of the nozzle. He was still a few steps away from the shed when the hose reached the end of its length. Clayton sighed and ran back toward the spigot to untangle the hose and give himself a bit more length. As he bent over, his finger pressed down on the nozzle, spraying the side of the house—including the electric meter. As the circuit continued getting doused, the lights in the previously bright house suddenly went dark.

"Aw, Sarge! Now we don't have any power," Clayton said. "Good job!"

Clayton's mom stormed back outside. "Clayton Anthony Peterson, what in the world is going on out here?! Sarge is barking like crazy, the power just went out, and—is the shed on *fire?*"

Clayton's head snapped around to face his approaching mother. His mouth silently open, he pointed at Sarge as, behind him, the roof collapsed into the burning shed.

Acknowledgments

To mom and dad, thank you for always supporting my creativity, from writing and broadcasting to guitar and drums. You've nurtured my curiosity in learning about the world and introduced me to travel and culture at a young age that built a foundation for the rest of my life.

To my sister Elizabeth, thank you for constantly recommending great reads, music, and shows that encourage me to push my writing.

To Haleigh, thank you for being a sounding board and putting up with my antics, including pacing around the room like a wackadoo when I'm taking a break from writing.

To Franxie and Merlin, thank you for being the best cuddlebugs a guy could ask for.

To my advanced readers, thank you for reading! Your input was incredibly helpful, and I don't know what I'd do without you. Special shoutouts to Craig Leener and Stacey Aaronson, who have been tremendously supportive and have shared their infinite wisdom on any question I've had along the way, big or small. I would highly recommend their books, since they are fantastic.

To Marco Pavia and your incredible team, thank you for guiding me through the process of launching a book, for killer designs, and dropping all kinds of helpful advice.

To my editors, Robert Kenney, Will Tyler, and Cecile Garcia, thank you for your thoroughly insightful suggestions, edits, and compliments. I learned a lot about both my own writing and other authors, and I truly appreciate your candor in helping make this book the best it can be.

To my friends, thank you for being there for me and making me smile, whether I've known you for 30 years or 30 days. Since I haven't had the same experiences with each of you, feel free to think back fondly on a memory we have together and chuckle softly, perhaps concluding with a sigh of satisfaction.

To my INK 1BHF, thank you for putting me in creative situations every day. Keeping my mind regularly challenged and firing on all cylinders is certainly not easy, but you've always been supportive, and I appreciate it more than words can express. That's probably not a good thing for a writer to say, yet here we are.

To my Austin foodie crew, thank you for embracing me with open arms. I couldn't have joined a more welcoming community. You've introduced me to so many good places to eat at and work from. Writing a book doesn't happen on an empty stomach, you know.

To my Burning Years boys, thank you for letting me run around and be silly onstage with you. Rock and roll is even more fun than I could have ever imagined.

To my "Good People, Cool Things" podcast guests, past, present, and future, thank you for taking the time to share your stories with me. I'm a better interviewer and storyteller because of this podcast, and that doesn't happen without your enthusiasm and effort.

To my Crisp Bounce Pass newsletter readers, thank you for the creative outlet. Your kind words never fail to make me smile, and your eagerness keeps me sharpening my chops — practicing written free throws, as it were — to continue delivering enjoyable writing.

Thank you, thank you, and thank you again. Y'all really are wonderful.

About the Author

Joey Held is a writer, podcaster, and author based in Austin, TX. He's covered marketing, sports, music, travel, and insurance for more than a decade, and is the founder of "Crisp Bounce Pass," a newsletter exploring the intersection of basketball and pop culture.

As a podcaster, Joey produces and hosts "Good People, Cool Things," featuring conversations with entrepreneurs, writers, musicians, and other creatives. He's also the producer and co-host of "Parks n Wrecked," a show about *Parks and Recreation* with a parks and rec employee, all while getting "wrecked" with local beverages.

Kind, But Kind of Weird: Short Stories on Life's Relationships is his first full-length collection of stories.

Made in the USA
Las Vegas, NV
13 February 2023